THE
ECLIPSE
THEATER

THE ECLIPSE THEATER

THE SUSPENSEFUL WORLD OF YOUR OWN IMAGINATION

BY
NASSER RABADI

ISBN: 978-0-9991475-0-4

DEDICATED TO MOM.

You walk down the street nearing your home. The sun has set, but the stars guide you with their light. A giant building appears to your right with giant glowing letters that spell out—

THE ECLIPSE THEATER

You're drawn in by the slow humming that calls to you from doors blown open by the wind. You walk inside and notice the humming getting faster; you follow it down a hallway and turn a corner, until you hear it coming from a door on your left.

The cold knob turns in your hand and it feels so surreal like you're in a dream looking through reality covered in a glass.

As you sit in the empty theater, a picture of blinding whiteness erupts onto the screen. The film is rolling. Sit down and enjoy the show!

STORY ONE:

SEQUOIA

The snow melted across the city of Kempton, Pennsylvania, as a warm wind fell upon it. Gorgeous rays of fresh sunlight shot down through high, thin clouds. Rissa Pearson walked down the block, taking in the nice weather. She was pretty, with long brown hair and equally brown eyes.

She arrived at Sequoia Gawlik's house at the end of the block. Something felt off. The doorbell—was it always old and cracked like that? She did not remember it being that way. And the door—it used to be light red, didn't it? But the blue paint was chipped, so it wasn't new.

"Hello?" Rissa said with another knock.

No answer.

She went for the knob. The faded brass knob turned gently in her hand and she stepped inside. Dust occupied the usually spotless house. Rissa coughed.

"Sequoia?" she called, and took another step.

She walked into the living room, where she saw an old '60s TV in the spot of the Smart TV. All the furniture was covered in white dust covers.

"Any—anybody here?"

Everything was just so odd; her stomach turned and her hair stood on end. Rissa had enough and ran out of the house. She took one more look at the house once she hit the sidewalk, then ran back to her home. She got to her bedroom, then jumped on the bed before even taking her shoes off. She reached for her phone—she had forgotten it on her nightstand—and tried to message Sequoia.

Sequoia's name did not appear when she searched for it. Rissa double-checked the spelling then attempted to find her on social media, but she still couldn't find her friend.

Strange. More than strange. Where is she? What's with everything at her house?

Since she couldn't find Sequoia, she called her friend Nevie for answers.

"Hey, Rissa! Good morning. Oh my gosh, did I tell you—"

"Where's Sequoia?" Rissa interrupted.

"Huh? Se-what?" replied Nevie, confused.

"Our friend... Sequoia..."

"Who's that? Do I know her?"

"Come on, Nevie. She only went on that New York trip with us that her mom took us on."

"Are you okay?" Nevie asked, sounding worried. "I don't know Sequoia or her mom or what New York trip you're talking about."

"How can I be okay when Sequoia's house is empty?" Rissa bit her lip. "I can't find her number or social media, and you don't even remember her mom or the New York trip!"

"Oh, I remember the New York trip," Nevie said, "but *my* mom is the one who took us that weekend, remember?"

Rissa hung up and threw her phone. Could she have imagined it all? No. She had known Sequoia for years—for most of her life. She couldn't have just imagined years' worth of friendship and memories.

Thinking she was crazy, she picked up her phone and Googled Sequoia Gawlik, but the results were not as she expected. The first page on Google was flooded with news articles; one headline read, "*Local Family Brutally Slaughtered.*"

Pain shot into Rissa's hands as she clicked the link; her stomach filled with fear. Was this the fate of her best friend? She read through the article but was baffled—it was dated November 3rd, 1970. Rissa felt confusion, fear, panic, and anxiety filling her all at once.

"This can't be right!" she yelled.

She got off her bed and looked under it for the shoe box of pictures. Most of the pictures in the box were from the New York trip. She flipped through every picture the group had taken together, but her beautiful blonde friend could not be seen with the group. She was behind them. Her blue eyes were now black with sullen bags below them. Her smile—which normally ran across her face— was nonexistent. In every picture, she could be seen creeping behind the group, watching them with her button-black eyes so fixated and evil, as if there were not a soul behind them.

She almost tripped on her own two feet in an unnecessary hurry, then put the pictures away and threw the box back under her bed.

***

Rissa didn't have much of an appetite the next morning at breakfast.

"Mom?" Rissa said, picking at her toast, "Can you drive me to Nevie's today, please? I'm meeting her and Sydney."

"Is all your homework done?" her dad asked.

"Yes, Dad," she replied.

"Sure, honey," her mom said.

They left after Rissa helped wash the dishes. The day wasn't as gorgeous as yesterday; the clouds overtook the sky and the wind was heavy, but that's Kempton weather—great one day, terrible the next.

"It won't be long until you have your permit," her mom said, "then I can teach you how to make this trip... you'll probably drive to Nevie's every day."

"Yeah," Rissa replied, staring out the window.

"It's weird how much you've grown up. My little baby girl, going on trips to New York, driving, picking out a college soon..."

Rissa turned to her mother, "Mom... sometimes all these things—it overwhelms me. Am I going crazy?"

"It's a very serious time in your life." Her mom smiled, almost laughing. "There are transitions and changes, but you find ways to deal with them."

They arrived at Nevie's house as Mrs. Pearson finished speaking.

"We can talk tonight. Have fun with your friends."

***

"So," Rissa said shyly, "neither of you remember Sequoia?"

"Nope," Nevie replied.

"Who?" asked Sydney.

"Guys, this doesn't make any sense." Rissa paced Nevie's room. "She was just here with us a few days ago, and now she's disappeared!"

"If you have a friend who's missing, you should call the cops," Sydney said.

"She's your friend too! Both of you! She went to New York with us last month and she lives two minutes from me," Rissa said. "I went to her house and it was all moldy and dust, and she's not there anymore."

Rissa walked to the corner of Nevie's room where some of Nevie's pictures from her Polaroid were hanging. She examined them, then, without taking her eyes off the pictures, said "She's right here in the background of all of these, watching us… except when we took these, she was with us."

Rissa moved out the way so Nevie and Sydney could look at the pictures. They both searched for the girl Rissa spoke of.

"I—I don't see anyone." Nevie said, almost sounding sad.

"Me neither," Sydney agreed.

Rissa looked back at the pictures. Sequoia was no longer in the backgrounds.

"What?" Rissa said. "How?"

***

Mrs. Pearson arrived to pick up Rissa early. Rissa felt the whole world was gonna explode; she was uneasy and almost felt her feet slip out from under her as she walked down the cement steps and to the car.

"How was your day, honey?" her mom asked.

"It was okay, mom, but I really wanna talk about what you were saying before I left... about finding—"

"Finding ways to deal with all the changes."

"Yeah..."

"Make two lists. The first is a to-do list, the second is a list of what's bothering you. The first will help clear your mind, the second will help you think of ways to change any situation that's bothering you, but don't forget that you have two parents who can help you with anything you need."

"I love you, Mom."

"I love you too, Rissa."

She went to sleep after she got home. One day went by, then two, and as they went by, Rissa hoped for some kind of new lead on Sequoia, but nothing happened. She researched the case she found on Google some more, but a week passed by without anything new. Then, a week became a month, and a month became two.

Rissa walked down the street to Sequoia's house just about every other day, hoping to discover her lost friend.

Today was no different. Rissa got up, threw on jeans and a t-shirt, and went for her morning walk. The stress of the whole debacle had weighed on her, both inside and out. The stress and depression played heavily on her face and in her eyes; she was losing her beauty.

From a distance, she could see Sequoia's house was normal now. Rissa ran as fast as she could the rest of the way to Sequoia's, then knocked rapidly on the door.

"Calm down! I'm coming!" a familiar voice on the other side of the door said.

The door opened, and Rissa greeted Sequoia with a nervous smile.

"Oh my God, can I come in?"

"Rissa? Everything okay?"

Sequoia led her into the house and they sat down on the big comfy couch in the living room.

"Sequoia, you've been gone for months! I kept stopping by but nobody was here and your house was dusty and ugly and old and—"

"Huh? What're you talking about? I've been here the whole time."

"You haven't been! Not even Nevie or Sydney remembered you!"

"Suuure they didn't."

"I can prove it."

Rissa took out her phone and typed Sequoia's name into Google. Nothing about the axe murders popped up. Rissa was nervous again.

"My mom texted me, I gotta go. Sorry."

Rissa left, trying to remain calm, wondering if this was all a joke or a prank or if she were crazy. Once the front door of Sequoia's house was shut behind her, she lost it. Tears flowed and she ran back to her home.

Rissa had to be sure of one thing: the photographs. She grabbed the box and sat down on her bed, terrified of what she might find. Her hands trembled. The silence grew louder—it was as though everything in the world had stopped dead, save for the beating of her own heart.

Sequoia was laughing and joking and having fun in every picture. She didn't look evil at all.

I'm perfectly sane. I'm perfectly sane.

She jumped when her phone rang. It was Sequoia.

Rissa answered, "Hello?"

"Rissa, I'm sorry, are you all right?"

"Yeah, why?"

"You seemed real out of it… I, uh, just wanna make sure you're okay… did you want to do something later, maybe have a sleepover?"

"Yeah—yeah, I'd like that. We haven't in a while."

***

A couple hours later, Rissa and Sequoia went for a walk along the biking trail behind Sequoia's house. The air was warm and the last bit of snow had melted two weeks ago, but Rissa wore a sweater anyway. Sequoia had her hair pulled back and wore a short-sleeved shirt and a skirt that went to her knees.

"Sometimes when I'm bored and it's nice out, I'll find a secret spot out here and read," Sequoia said. "You know how relaxing it is to read in nature?"

"I'm not much of a reader," Rissa replied.

"So what's been on your mind?" Sequoia asked. "Nature isn't just the best place to read, it's also the best place to talk."

"If I said what I—if I said what was on my mind, you'd be *so* annoyed."

"Are—are you still on that 'you've been gone for a month' or whatever thing? Rissa, I'm right here and I'm not going anywhere."

Rissa sighed, "We can talk about this or we can talk about good things. I would rather talk about good things."

"Then tell me something good." Sequoia said, taking in the beauty that surrounded them.

"Uh, school's been good."

"Really, Rissa? The first 'good' thing that comes to your mind is school?"

"Sorry, I wasn't sure what to say… I guess with all the stress I'm under, it's hard to think of something good."

"There'll always be some good."

"Well, what can I say?" Rissa said. "Along with stressful, everything has been dull."

"Come on, you don't sound like the Rissa I know. Aren't you always positive?"

"Even the positive can get depressed."

"I'm sorry, Rissa."

"It's okay, it's not your fault. I'm just too stressed… I just need to clear my head."

"What's bothering you?"

"My head's just filled with too many things." Rissa sighed.

They walked back to Sequoia's house. Things seemed normal to Rissa and any thought of Sequoia disappearing or being dead faded from her mind. She played videos games with Sequoia while they listened to music for hours.

At the end of the night, Rissa gathered her clothes to shower. The water was lukewarm—she was probably the only person on the planet who didn't like hot water. She let the water run over her and wash the stress away.

She put on her favorite pink pajamas, and when she walked out of the bathroom, she stepped right onto dust. Sequoia was gone. Mr. and Mrs. Gawlik were gone. The house was old, dusty, and moldy. The '60s TV and the white dust cover sheets were back. The house was ancient.

Rissa bolted back to her house, fearing that somehow she'd slip away from existence like Sequoia did if she stayed there any longer. She left behind the clothes she'd brought with her, pausing only to grab her shoes.

She sat down on her bed, ready to look up the articles again. Sweat dripped down her forehead and saturated into her eyebrows. She had this silly feeling in her gut that wouldn't go away. She saw that her thoughts were correct as the page loaded and she saw the familiar articles, all about how Sequoia was chopped to death on November 3rd, 1970. And when she checked the godforsaken box under her bed, she was also correct—Sequoia and her evil eyes were behind the group, watching from a distance. Rissa was sick to her stomach.

An hour later, she fell asleep. She woke up a couple times with a nosebleed but brushed it off and fell asleep. Things were becoming unusual. This carried on into the coming week and into the rest of the month. She brushed off the nosebleeds—those were explainable; but the unexplainable was the tiredness she felt and the pains that flickered inside her body. Sometimes it was a mental aching; sometimes it would be pain in her hands and legs and even her sides. Sometimes it lasted for a few moments; other times it lasted a day. Rissa lost her appetite. She couldn't explain it but felt that it was all happening because of Sequoia. Maybe it was just the stress weighing on her, maybe it was something more, but she felt herself going crazy. No matter what she did or tried to do, it felt as though she was stuck between two realities— the first one where Sequoia existed and the second one where Sequoia died before Rissa was even born, when her parents were just toddlers.

***

Then one day the pictures in Rissa's box were back to normal and the links on Google were gone. Sequoia was back. Her parents were back too, and the house was normal once again. Rissa hurried down the block that morning, and found Sequoia reading outside.

"How are you doing this?" Rissa said, not even close to Sequoia's house yet.

"Doing what?" Sequoia replied once Rissa was closer. She shut her book and looked up to her friend.

"Where have you been?" Rissa was nearly screaming.

"You're scaring me," Sequoia said.

"Your whole house turns to dust, and you're just gone for weeks! You disappear from the group photos and become someone watching us in the background!"

"Rissa—"

"How on earth are you doing this?"

"Rissa what the he—"

"*Stop doing this to me! Just stop!*"

Sequoia stood up. "Get—get away!"

Sequoia rushed inside and slammed the door in Rissa's face.

"Sequoia! Sequoia, listen to me!" Rissa pounded on the door.

Rissa tried the knob a few more times, even though it was locked. She kept knocking and knocking and trying to turn the knob. Then, as if it were never locked, the door swung open, and Rissa fell through the doorframe onto dust.

***

Rissa was out of breath when she sat down at her desk. Her mind couldn't process what had happened. The house didn't change before her eyes, it just... was. The house didn't morph, there was no in-between stage. The house was dusty and run down, but it was unexplainable how she didn't see it change into that from a normal house.

She went from her desk to her bed, then got the box from under it. She sorted the pictures into two piles: New York was the first pile, the second was "other". She took the stack of New York pictures and spread them out across the blue carpet. Sequoia was evil in each one.

Rissa took a picture of each New York photograph. *This time, when she comes back, I'll have proof.*

And to her surprise, it wasn't long before she'd be offering Sequoia proof—she was back the next day, book and all. Rissa didn't notice her from her morning walk,

Rissa noticed her because she was looking for her. She'd check the house every day for the rest of her life if she had to, she needed to get to the bottom of this.

Rissa pulled out her phone as she walked up to Sequoia, whose nose was practically always buried in the latest novel she was enjoying.

Sequoia noticed her coming closer and looked up, "Oh, hey, Rissa. You, uh, feeling better?"

Rissa didn't acknowledge Sequoia's words, she just shoved her phone in Sequoia's face.

"Explain these!"

Sequoia looked down and examined what was on the screen. She swiped to the side, then spied again, and looked up to Rissa, confused.

"You wanted to show me a picture of a picture?" Sequoia asked.

"What?" Rissa said, not in reply to Sequoia, but to what she saw on the screen.

The picture of a picture from the New York trip was a normal picture now. There was no creepy Sequoia. Rissa could not believe her eyes. She searched for the screen shots of the articles about Sequoia's death, but they were all missing. There was not a single shred of evidence that Sequoia was dead or looking evil. Rissa felt that all too familiar pain shooting inside her body.

It can't be. It can't be. It can't be. She's dead! Sequoia is dead! How can she be here now when she died all those years ago? I know it's true, it has to be!

She left Sequoia in a hurry. Back in her room, her thoughts turned to cries and she sobbed quietly to herself, careful so that her parents would not hear her. She curled up in bed, holding in a scream.

I have to stay at her house until I see it switch to dust with my own eyes. I won't take my eyes off of her, I'll see her disappear for myself.

"Maybe I can play this whole thing off as a joke," Rissa said aloud to her empty room.

After half an hour her eyes stopped being so red and her strained throat wasn't hurting as bad. She left the house again to go down the block to Sequoia's. Rissa's heart was struck with horror at the sight of the chipped paint on the door and that nasty, broken doorbell. The windows were dusty and dirty and hard to see through. Even the grass now was old and dead. The house had gotten worse—much worse.

Rissa knew in her heart that nobody would answer her, but she knocked on the door anyway.

"Sequoia? You home?"

But nobody answered her. Rissa checked to see if the door was unlocked, and it was. She took a step inside. She was greeted by dust once more, but this time something else was in there, in the middle of the emptiness: a warm, bloody axe.

She wanted to make sure Sequoia and her parents were okay; her bravery almost got the better of her, but then she realized whoever had used the bloody axe might still be around, and if Sequoia hadn't been dead for decades, she certainly was now.

She ran away from Sequoia's—running away from Sequoia's almost felt routine now—and back to her house. She dialed the non-emergency police number and requested to stay anonymous. The minutes ticked by quickly, and she watched from her window until the police arrived.

She watched the police knock on the Gawliks' door. They knocked and knocked and Rissa waited and waited.

No one's answering; they'll have to see what I saw.

Suddenly the door swung open and Mrs. Gawlik answered the police. Rissa's jaw dropped—she was puzzled, *Sequoia was just gone, how is she back now?*—and she watched them talk for a few moments before they went inside. She nervously glanced out the window until the police left a few minutes later. Rissa waited a couple hours, giving the Gawliks time to cool down, then walked back over.

There was a gloomy cloud above Rissa, and she felt like an idiot.

Sequoia was sitting on the steps, bewitched by the book she was reading.

"Sequoia?"

Sequoia looked into Rissa's sad, brown eyes, then angrily said, "Thanks for that."

"I'm sorry! I saw the axe!"

"What axe?"

"I opened the door and it was in the middle of your house."

Sequoia rolled her eyes.

"Something is going on!" Rissa said, trying not to sound crazy.

"Oh, cut it out. You're crazy. I'm not dead and my parents aren't dead and we're right here in front of you. Everyone's been talking about what you've been saying."

"Sequoia—"

"Don't 'Sequoia' me. How could you go around playing this weird game? It makes me uncomfortable. We're supposed to be friends."

"We are—we are friends!"

"Then please stop saying I'm dead or disappearing or whatever. Just please..." Sequoia got up and opened the door, "just leave me alone for now. I need space. Please."

Panic struck Rissa. What could she do at this point? Continue living in fear? Seeing her best friend once every... who knows how often, and just ignoring the puzzle lying in front of her? No. She couldn't let this go.

The next day, Sequoia's home was still there, but Rissa did not see Sequoia on the front steps.

She probably knew I'd see her on the front steps and bother her... maybe she's somewhere off the biking trail.

Rissa walked along the biking trail until it split into two paths. The one on the left went straight ahead and the one on the right curved up a little hill. Rissa went on the right path. She was only a little out of breath by the time she got to the top of the hill and saw Sequoia reading on the bench, an ice-cold bottle of water at her side.

"Can—can we talk?" Rissa asked while catching her breath.

Sequoia sighed, and without looking up from her book, replied, "You walked all the way here... so I suppose we can."

"I'm sorry I haven't been myself. I'm sorry I found the worst way to deal with things."

"Rumors are how you deal with things, Rissa?"

Rissa was on the verge of tears, "I know I sound like a jerk."

"This really hurt me." Sequoia said, "Especially because it's coming from my best friend."

"I can't say sorry enough."

"You don't have to," Sequoia said, "I'll be okay."

"I really wanna still be friends."

"And so do I. I don't wanna give up on our friendship."

"Me too."

"If you stop… uh, stop trying to freak me out, and you stop calling the cops… then I'll look past everything that happened lately."

"I'll never speak of it again."

They hugged.

"What're you up to tonight?" Sequoia asked.

Rissa replied, "Cramming for Monday."

"That's what Sunday is for. We haven't had a sleep over in so long, why don't we—"

"Sure, I'll just have to get some stuff from my house first."

Rissa walked away; Sequoia stayed a little longer to read.

Sequoia believes every word of my apology. I almost feel sorry for her, but I have to know what's happening. I have to know if Sequoia is real or not. Is she part of my imagination?

***

Empty pizza boxes rested on the floor in Sequoia's room next to the TV that night. The girls played video games and listened to music while they played.

"What movie do you want to see?" Sequoia asked.

"I'm too tired to pick," replied Rissa.

"It has been a long day."

"I'm glad we had this sleepover," Rissa yawned, "and I'm sorry again about... everything."

"Everything's totally fine."

Rissa stood up and stretched. The clock on the wall in front of her struck midnight, and she felt a shift in the air. Something strange was beginning.

She realized that tonight was now November 3rd. The music coming from Sequoia's phone had suddenly stopped. Any trace of the PlayStation was gone, and so was Sequoia.

All that remained was dust, and the bloody axe that fell from Rissa's hands.

STORY TWO:

WHERE AM I?

Where am I?

I wake up under the warmth of covers that cling to me. I look around, but there isn't much to see in the room I'm in.

Who am I?

I hear a simple melody of a guitar; I don't know what the song is, but it's refreshing and calming and coming from somewhere near me... but where? I wish I knew where I was or who I am.

I move the covers and step out of bed. Colors flutter in my eyes and heat rushes through my head. I'm so dizzy I fall over.

Just breathe, just breathe slowly. In and out.

I finally get to the door. I step outside, but I'm still confused. I see a man at the end of the hall, wearing a uniform. He stares at me, then looks away. I follow the sound of the guitar to the room next to mine. I put my ear to the door and ignore how cold it is.

Knock, knock, knock.

My knuckles hit the door quietly. A boy lets me in without saying anything. He sits down on his bed and resumes playing his guitar. I sit across from him, and I'm still confused.

"Who am I?" I asked him, "I can't remember who I am or where I am."

"Just another person in this basket of crazies," he tells me.

"I'm sorry?"

"You don't remember? You're more gone than I thought... not that I know you well."

"Can you please stop being vague?"

He fidgets with his guitar pick before replying, "This is the Carpenter Sanitarium. This is where crazy people come and never leave. You're the new girl, Julia. You joined my group therapy just yesterday. Don't you remember?"

"No. I—I've never seen you or this place before in my life."

He went back to playing his guitar. The noise it made was beautiful, but I got tired of it. My head had been pounding since I woke up, and I was beyond exhausted, confused, and lost.

"If I really was in your group therapy, did I say why I was here? I'm not crazy... and why can't I remember a thing?"

"I don't got all the answers, and I don't know why you think I got 'em all."

We both went silent for minutes while he played more music on his guitar.

"Sorry for all the questions," I rubbed the left side of my head, "but why do you play your guitar so late into the night? Doesn't it bother anyone?"

"Most people are asleep and won't hear," he said, in rhythm with the tune, "and I can't not play it. It keeps them away. It's the only thing that stops them from taking me. The things under my bed. They come out at night, that's why I have to stay up and play. If I don't, they'll come take me. It sounds like nails on a chalkboard to them."

I pulled my legs up from the floor and onto his bed. I didn't believe him, but at this point, I wasn't gonna take any chances. I stayed there for an hour listening to his music, neither of us saying a word, but then I left to my room. I told him goodnight. All he responded with was, "My name is Collin."

***

I jolted awake. Someone was banging on my door.

"Uhh?" was all I knew to respond with.

A nurse walked in and gave me medicine. I wanted to spit it out, but it tasted like bubblegum and was so sweet I swallowed it without thinking. When I saw her with the pills, I had slightly suspected that maybe these were why I couldn't remember anything, but I didn't forget anything since last night, so that couldn't be it.

I put my hair in a bun and changed into what clothes I could find. I didn't know where to go or what I was to do, but I left my room. The hallway was filled with people, and anxiety took over and I panicked and ran. I ran until I got to another hallway, hoping to escape the crowd of people, but this one was full too. I turned into another; this one was empty. I was curious, so I walked down it, but the dust and emptiness made me feel sick; I could feel myself ready to puke at any second. So I turned into another hallway. There were so many... did it ever end?

I reached a stairway and started to walk up, but stopped halfway. There was nothing up there—the staircase ended midair. My hands shook on the railing as I stepped back down. Beyond that, I saw doors as small as bricks, I saw doors as large as houses. Most of the lights were normal, but some lights were flashing green.

I found myself in one hallway that swirled into the shape of a snail's shell. I was so drawn into this winding pattern that I kept going around it, my mind feeling more worry with each step, and my mind too curious to turn around. The end of this hallway had a chair. Only a chair.

I turned around to leave but the way I came from was gone. I turned back around to the chair, thinking that perhaps I missed something else. Either I had, or it only appeared after I turned my back, but there was a new hallway now, a hallway that for once had an "EXIT" sign at the end. I felt hope flash through me for the first time since I awoke last night.

I don't think anyone has ever moved faster than I had in that moment. In a blink, I was outside the door that the "EXIT" sign hovered over. I was stunned by what I saw: flowers taller than me and extending as far as an ocean. I walked up to a purple one and felt it. It gave me a feeling of relaxation. Sure, I didn't know who I was or where I was, but this flower under my finger told me everything was all right, it told me I didn't have reason to worry anymore.

I turned to walk in the other direction. Each flower was unique. I didn't see two at all that were the same. And the smell, oh God, the smell—it was better than baked cookies. I sat down under the shade of a flower, and looked to the sky.

The sky didn't look back. Rain hit my face. I shrieked because it was so unexpected. Then the winds grew, and my clothes danced in the breeze and battered against the dirt of the ground. I tried to get up, but it was suddenly freezing and I almost couldn't—the shivers overtook me.

When I got up, the sky was all darkness, as though it was vaporous ink that covered a paper sky. The rains poured in little black droplets. I thought I was gonna die. I looked over and the sanitarium was gone.

Oh, God! Oh, God! Oh, God!

My vision spiraled and I was embraced by a loud humming noise.

HUM, HUM, HUM!

***

I woke up in a hallway that was more bizarre than any hallway I had seen before—and that was saying a lot. The floor had white lines that traced from random points in one wall to random points in another. The floor was made of wood, but wasn't flat—sections of the floor made obscure holes and textures in the ground. If I took any step without looking, I'd certainly fall on my ass. Light shone in from a snake-shaped window and I was taken aback. Wasn't it just terrible outside? Freezing winds and raining black ink? The oddest part, however, was the maddening optical illusions carved into the stone walls— the shapes spun in my tired mind relentlessly, and as my mind was ready to give, I noticed Collin standing over me.

"Col-Collin?" I said. "What's going on?"

"Heh." He laughed. "Oh Julia. I told you before that nobody gets out of here. What did you see when you went out? I went out once. You'll be glad I found you. It's different for everyone out there."

"Different? Different for everyone? What?"

"This isn't a normal place. We're drifting far away from reality. We're drifting in a pocket away from known existence. Outside of here... outside of here is a disk that we're on. You get four feet in any direction before you fall off and die. It's enchanted to show us something happy, and if you stay long enough, it goes to shit and you'll die. There's no escape."

"No wonder you're in here, you're crazy!"

"There's a reason you're in here, too. We are all crazy."

"We're not floating... we're not in some pocket dimension, Collin."

"After all you've seen here, that's the least believable thing? Seriously?"

I couldn't reply. Dozens of voices in my head spoke to me.

You are a cray little bitch.

You're a fucking psycho!

No, I'm normal, I'm normal.

Sounds to me like you're trying to convince yourself you're normal.

I'm normal, goddammit, I'm normal.
You are a crazy little bitch.

"Come on, Julia, you've missed breakfast, but we might still make it to group therapy on time."

***

I sat next to Collin at a large, round table. There were four other people, plus the man in charge. I didn't know what to call him. He was on Collin's right. A spiral staircase stood behind me, leading to an upper level that had a library. The walls had the design of a mixed-up Rubik's cube, except it took up the entirety of the ten-foot walls, and the 'pieces' kept shifting, making annoying combinations and triggering more and more anxiety and annoyance in my mind.

The man turned to me, and for the first time, somebody in the room spoke. "Miss Julia, how're you liking it here at Carpenter? Any thoughts on yesterday's session?"

"Well, uh, what is your name, sorry?" I asked.

"Julia, are you okay? You know my name, you met me when you checked in."

"I—but I never checked in! I woke up last night to find myself in this strange place. What am I doing here? Collin told me I had gotten here yesterday, but I don't remember ever coming here. I don't know where I am, I don't even remember *who* I am."

"Julia, who's Collin?"

I pointed to the boy right next to me, "He's Collin."

"What?" Collin and this man said in unison, then Collin continued speaking, "Collin? My name's not Collin, and I haven't even spoken to you since we introduced ourselves at yesterday's session. I'm Braden."

"Braden?" I asked. A bad feeling plagued my stomach. "But last night you told me you were Collin, and I called you Collin today you didn't object. Is your name Braden?"

"Yes, my name is Braden, but I haven't talked to you since our session yesterday."

"And I am Doctor Nicholas Midler. Tell me, Julia, did you take your medicine today?"

"Yeah—yeah, I did."

"You sure?"

"Yes…"

"Okay, Julia." He turned to face everyone. "Sorry about that little distraction, everybody. Now, let's get on with today's group therapy session."

Weird.

Very weird.

"Why am I here?" I spoke before he could get another word in. "I don't need therapy or whatever. I'm normal."

"We eventually believe our own lies." He spoke without missing a beat, then went over to a blackboard I didn't notice before and started to write. *I DON'T NEED THERAPY,* he wrote in all caps.

"You're a very troubled girl, Julia, and being a compulsive liar is one of your problems." His gaze broke from my eyes and he turned to Braden and the other four people. "Class, Julia keeps telling herself she doesn't need therapy. I think she's trying to make herself feel a little less guilty about what she's done to deserve being here. A way to cope. How many of you think Julia could get beyond this and cope in healthy ways if she really tried?"

Everyone raised their hands. I wasn't sure to raise mine or not.

"Look at that, Julia, they all think it's possible. You can't help yourself until you admit there's a problem."

"But there isn't a problem! I want to get out of here. I *need* to get out of here. His name is Collin, not Braden! And I am not crazy, I am not crazy, I am a normal girl!"

"Class," Doctor Midler said, "this is why we have groups in Carpenter and don't always do one-on-one sessions. Julia is struggling, but she will be supported by other people suffering from similar things. You'll all learn from each other. You can—and will—learn from a doctor, yes, but this way you don't feel so isolated. Julia, you'll find comfort in your friends here, and I'm sure they all feel what you feel right now."

But they didn't.

Could they?

"Well, I think I'd be—I'd feel better if I knew what you all struggle with," I said. "Why are you all here?"

"We did this yesterday for Julia, but let's do it again today. Introduce yourselves, everyone." Doctor Midler instructed.

"I'm Roberta." A girl spoke while cracking her fingers. I noticed three of them missing. "I'm here because I am sick. I have autophagia, I like to…"

Roberta started to cry, and the boy next to her patted her back, then he said, "It's fine, Roberta, you don't have to finish."

There was an awkward silence before that same boy spoke again, "I'm Mark. I used to be like you, thinking I don't need—don't need t-to—to be—to be here. But Doctor Midler has helped me se-see th-that I do. I do nee-need to be here."

Vague.

The next girl just stayed silent.

"I'm Timmy," the last person before Braden (or was he Collin?) spoke. "My—my senses are distorted. Sometimes I feel like I'm Alice in Wonderland. I don't like the hallways. Or this room. It all hurts me too much. Whatever you see on these walls—"

I was annoyed by the walls too, especially the ones in this room.

"It's ten- it's ten times worse for me."

"Uh, I'm Braden. You called me Collin... sometimes I feel fine, but I'm paranoid. I always knew someone was watching me, ever since I was a kid. That's why I learned to play my guitar, because it keeps them away. They're watching me, and they hate the guitar. To them, it sounds like nails on a blackboard."

This is crazy, I sorta already knew that about... Braden? Collin? He told me that same thing, the nails on a blackboard thing. What is this? Where am I?

"Now you." Doctor Midler nodded toward me.

"I'm Julia...." I didn't know what to say. "I guess I don't know what's wrong with me."

"Hey, we're all here to improve. Just be honest with yourself," Mark said.

Mark seemed nice.

I guess I just like denying what's wrong." I quickly made up a lie.

"Hey, it's a start," he said.

The rest of therapy was awkward. I kept silent through most of it. These people... they were truly crazy. I knew I wasn't crazy, I knew that for a fact, but all of these people were... I wished I knew what they thought of me. What did they think was wrong with me?

Everyone started to leave. I walked into the hallway, acting normal, but I didn't know where to go. Then I remembered that Braden/Collin's room was next to mine, so I followed him. The walk was long. I passed so many strange things.

I was in a hallway that twisted on its side. I twisted so that I was walking literally sideways, then on the ceiling. I couldn't believe it. I was gasping with every step because the pure wonder of it all took away my breath, and I was nervous— but who wouldn't be? This hallway didn't have light bulbs, it had flying orbs of light. I reached out to touch one and it felt like I was touching soft electricity.

I lost Collin—I mean Braden? I lost Braden on my walk back because a girl with long dark hair stopped me.

"I know you," she said.

"You do?" I replied, "What is my name? Is it—am I Julia? I think I'm Julia."

"Huh? You're Lucy." She laughed.

Was I Lucy?

"Am I?"

"Don't you remember? I showed you around after you checked in yesterday."

"I don't remember."

"Oh, I think I get it, you're not Lucy right now, you're Julia."

"What?"

"It's okay, Julia. How are you today, Julia? I'm Nancy, nice to meet ya!"

"Uh, I'm not too good. I don't know how to get back to my, uh, room."

"You just keep going straight."

I looked down the hallway then back to her but she was gone. I didn't know where she went. Odd. I continued down the hallway.

The next hallway had holes in every wall. Through them, I caught glimpses of the flowers I saw earlier. How I loved the flowers. My curiosity got the better of me, I had to see them again. I put my eyes to one hole and a slimy eye looked back at me. I jumped away from it and cried.

My tears were my only companion for the rest of my walk. I got into a hallway that looked like the first hallway I remembered stepping into. I should've looked at the number on my door before I left, because now I wasn't even sure which room was mine.

But that was nothing new, right? I was getting used to not knowing. I didn't know if I was Julia or Lucy, I didn't know if there was anything wrong with me, I didn't know if that boy was Braden or Collin, I didn't know which room was mine, I didn't even know where I was or how to leave.

"Oh, I'll never find my room," I said out loud.

Then a door opened.

I peeked inside and it looked close enough. I got on the bed then fell asleep.

***

I woke up so damn hungry, but a little less confused. I still didn't have answers to my questions, but at least my questions seemed finite. At least I didn't have more memory loss. My head hurt a little less, too.

I stared at the ceiling, then realized I was listening to that same melody from Braden's guitar. I walked over to his room and opened the door. I walked over to his bed and sat down where I had sat down the last time. He never looked up.

"You're back, Lucy. Couldn't sleep?"

"Lucy? Braden, you told me my name was Julia."

"Braden? Julia? Lucy, I told you last time you were in here, my name is Collin."

"Collin? That's what I said when you told me it was Braden."

"I don't know what you're talking about."

"Does anybody?"

He continued to play the guitar.

"Your guitar keeps your demons away, it keeps you sane. Can it keep me sane? Can anything?"

"Depends, what's your problem, babe?"

"Memory problems, I guess," I said. "I keep getting confused, thinking one thing is another."

"I don't know, have you seen Doctor Midler yet? He's a swell guy."

"I—you were—you were there with me when I did! We had group therapy together!"

"Yeah, we did the first time. You didn't show today."

"I did show!"

"No."

"Yes."

"Collin, please, Collin, you need to help me! My brain is so all over the place."

"Calm down and listen. Listen to the strings."

So I did. I lay down on his bed. He didn't seem to mind, but I don't know if he even noticed. Great, another thing to be unsure about. He just kept playing, and I listened. The melody he made was charming; it did a great job of relaxing me. He played for hours, all through the night and I just listened, not wanting to sleep, wanting to know how the melody to his song ended.

"That's all I got," Collin said once he finished playing.

"That was marvelous. You're so wonderful, Collin." I said.

"Collin? Julia, I told you, I'm Braden."

Enough was enough.

"I am so sorry, Braden. I'll try not to mix it up again. I'll see you in the group session later."

I left the room with no intention to go to the group therapy session. I found the door again that had the "EXIT" sign hanging right above it. I walked out and avoided being hypnotized by the flowers. I waited long enough and was consumed by the cold and wind. The rain of ink fell upon me. I didn't pay it much attention, I just looked out in front of me until I saw it, and it was true—there was only four feet of room in front of me, and then the edge. Four wonderful feet and I'd be free. Four wonderful feet and I'd fall into a soup of mazarine blues mixing with waves of wine and broken light.

I walked to the edge, and I jumped.

STORY THREE:

THE GIRL IN THE BOX

Of the many mysteries in life, this one was perhaps the most unexplainable. One day, Lauren was trapped in a silver box that shined on the outside, but the inside was a dark abysmal void to her berry-blue eyes. There was space for Lauren to lie down inside the box, or to sit halfway up if she wanted to. Her arms and legs had half an inch of wiggle room, so they wouldn't be totally stiff. She had only been there for a few hours; her body didn't ache as much as her mind did.

You'll get out of this soon, I know you will, she calmed herself.

No, you're gonna die in here, a new, unfamiliar voice in her head said. The voice was unrecognizable.

You deserve it, Lauren. You know what you did to deserve it, don't you? You're gonna be stuck in here for eternity, you know that? And do you know how long eternity lasts?

No—no, I don't know what I did, I don't know why I deserve it, and I don't know how long eternity is.

You stand on the beach Clearwater, Florida, and pick up a grain of sand. You fly about four hours to Moonstone Beach in California. You must set down that first grain of sand, fly all the way back to Florida, and grab one more single grain of sand. You keep doing this until you've completely transferred all the sand. That's eternity, my darling.

My darling? Who are you?

You know who I am, Lauren.

But I don't know! Who are you? What is this?

The new voice in her head disappeared, and she was left with her own thoughts and misery. A small humming started to sound from all around her. She thought she was crazy, and when she tried to shift her position in the box, searching for just a bit of relief, she found that it had become an inch shorter—possibly less than an inch, but definitely shorter. Her body tired, regardless of the change, and her eyelids shut as deep sleep fell upon her.

She woke up to that deep, ugly, new voice in her head, *Wake up, Lauren.*

Huh? Why am I still in here?

You know damn well why you're in here, Lauren.

Listen, wouldn't it just make things easier if you just told me why I'm here? Explain to me. Talk to me. We can work it out, whatever it is... I promise.

It's too late to work it out, Lauren. It's too late to promise anything.

The box tightened around her, limiting her movements. Her small torso no longer had the space to sit up. Her arms pressed tight against her sides, her knees uncomfortable from being stretched out straight. The feeling in her upper arms disappeared; pain shots in sparks from her hands, stopping near her elbows.

Who would survive this? You're hungry and tired and your body is cramping, she told herself. Any hope she once had was gone.

You're seeing things my way, Lauren, the strange voice replied. *You deserve it.*

But how—but why do I deserve it?

Lauren, oh Lauren, you demand the truth but you refuse to be honest.

We're getting nowhere! Just tell me! This is annoying. I'm angry and confused and I'm hurt, just tell me what the fuck is going on!

Hum, hum, hum! The only reply was that creepy hum climbing into her ear like a spider.

The box became tinier. The first couple changes were tolerable, but soon her spine was bent and her legs pushed into her hip. Her back and neck muscles pounded with fear. She lost all the feeling in her arms, save for the sparks of pain that still found a way through. Panic traced her body.

Are you there? Lauren asked the other voice in her head. *Please let me go!*

No answer, just the humming that would never stop. It drove her mad. She would claw her ears out if she could move her arms. She begged and pleaded for the humming to end, but it didn't. It never would.

Lauren slipped in and out of consciousness. The pain riddled into her body was more than she could bear; she desperately needed to find a way out.

She screamed into the void and gave herself a headache. Her throat was strained, so she paused, then as if she weren't in control, screamed again just as loudly. Her face felt hot, and she screamed and screamed again, absolutely sure that somebody would hear her. But nobody could. She shut her eyes tight then let out another wail. Grief filled her, and her head pounded. She cried with the subsequent screams until her voice finally gave out, and she could scream no more.

Hours passed, but for all she knew it could've been months. It seemed that in this box, her body didn't depend on food or water to live. She felt the effects of being starved and dehydrated—her eyes were sunken and her heart beat rapidly while her stomach growled and her thick, dry tongue hit the roof of her mouth—but she was alive through every speck of torture.

You know what I think, Lauren? That godawful voice appeared. She dreaded hearing it.

What? What do you think?

I think the human body can be a pretty painful thing to live in, don't you agree?

Uh, I—I guess so. Painful is just an understatement at this point.

Since it can be so painful, why don't we just cut it open and get you out?

Screams escaped her mouth before, "What do you mean?" ever had the chance to. The box shrunk again, pushing both femurs through her hip and snapping them. Flesh spread apart all around her body. Skin snapped around her neck and drained out gallons of blood. An energetic pump of feeling and pain spun through her arms where she had lost all feeling. The sounds of cracking bones were all that she could hear.

I would rather die!

Hum, hum, hum! Hum, hum, hum!

Her blood seemed endless; it soaked into her clothes and hair and tugged her down. The box shrunk and kept shrinking. Lauren ran out of space, but that didn't stop the box from getting smaller. As it shrank, she could feel every vein snap and every tendon tear and every wave of blood leave her body. The box—if she could somehow find it to measure—was now a two-foot cube. Lauren was still alive, sinking deeper and deeper into the thick, red ocean of blood, hearing nothing but hums.

Hum, hum, hum!

STORY FOUR:

A DREAM OF DEATH

I'm submerged in water, yet somehow I breathe. The thick water brims to the ceiling and has engulfed my entire house. I drown, but I live. I see the remaining inch of space clearly—and I know the water won't stop growing until it's gone; it feels so alive.

Something is in the water with me, but I can't see it. It's dragging me down, down to the bottom of this watery hell. There's more pressure surrounding my body, still drowning, yet I'm alive—and now I'm stuck to the floor as though I'm a tile glued in place.

The doll appears three feet away from me. There's a demon in the doll—I just know it. The doll stares at me, he's the reason I'm drowning. Why can't I wake up?

His fabric legs bend like a human's would, and he moves towards me. I can't move, every part of me is stuck. He stares at me and comes closer; his painted eyes—unaffected by the water—are fixated on me, looking through me. They're demented and evil and sickening. The deep black paint is filthy and I feel if I touched one, I'd fall straight through into another realm.

Why is he doing this to me? He's the reason I'm drowning so deep and—oh God. He's so much closer to me now. The waters are holding him back but they're no match for him. He's inches away and I can't move. I'm stuck here like a brick cemented in a wall. The water of my dreams won't let me escape.

His hand reaches out to me. I'm still stuck. I beg myself to wake up, to move, but it won't make a damn difference, will it? Because this time he's as close as he's ever come, and he's about to touch me. The centimeters between him and me are shrinking. I'm terrified, and I cannot move as his hand is but a hair away…

And then he touches me.

***

Deep in Redwick, California, Miranda woke up from a dream—the ones that had haunted her for almost exactly a year. Each dream was different, yet equally terrifying; she never had a moment of peace. They all started when the doll showed up—and she was so terrorized from the dreams that she did not even remember who gave her the doll in the first place.

She woke up in a fit of coughs that turned into cries—and her three young sons watching from down the hallway winced when she did. They were terrified, and were clueless what to do about their mother's condition.

"What's wrong with Mom?" the youngest one whispered.

"I don't know, I just hope she gets better," replied the oldest one.

"What if we got her a doctor?" the youngest one asked.

The middle child replied, "There's nothing to fix."

And perhaps the middle child was correct; maybe there was nothing to fix. Perhaps some things can't be fixed.

At that moment, the rains began. The sky was a cryptic sable filled with many clouds. Miranda shot up in bed at the sound of rain. Her hands passed through her messy hair and covered her eyes.

Her eyes were stuck on the doll across the room. It always sat there, the children never dared to touch it. Miranda herself never touched it. The doll lived in its little spot across the room, always sitting there, never touched, and never moving unless in her dreams.

"Make it stop!" she shouted. "Make the doll stop! Make the rain stop!"

The boys froze. They listened to their mother scream as they had so often done.

"It's the doll! It's the doll! Why does it do this?"

But the doll just sat there and the rains poured heavily. She dug her fingers deep into her hair and screamed and shook as if she were possessed. Her insanity grew with the falling rain, and so did her children's fright—the boys cried and hid in their rooms, but could not escape the uneasy feeling that accompanied Miranda's fits.

The rest of the day faded away, but the rain did not. The rain persisted until Miranda slipped into another dream.

***

I wake up in bed and the doll is gone. I move the covers away, and soft air floats around me. I feel fine. I walk across the room and out the door.

The boys!

Where are the boys? Does—does the doll have them?

I walk around the house. They're not watching TV, they're not at the kitchen table, I don't know where they could be. I peek out the window, yet still I don't see my boys. Where are my precious little boys?

I breathe in and out with every step I take up the stairs. My boys will be fine, my boys will be fine. Everything is okay.

I'm in the upstairs hallway. They should be in their rooms. Of course they're in their rooms. They must *be in their rooms. I call their names from where I stand, but nobody answers me. They're not there. I even call to the doll. I finally open that first damned door and find an empty room. My oldest boy isn't there, and I slam the door shut. The tears want to flow but they don't.*

I walk to my second child's room. I knock. No reply. I try to open the door but the knob doesn't turn. I bang on the door and suddenly it flings open, and I am met with emptiness once more. I was sure they would be in here because it was locked, but my boys are nowhere to be found.

My baby boy's door is wide open. I see nothing at first—just an empty room filled with light. No bed or dresser or spilled Legos and blocks. Then the boys come into view, appearing first as faint apparitions until they become something more. They're back. My boys are back.

The youngest is on his bed, his older brothers are on the floor. I kneel by my older boys. I feel their pulses and I see them breathing. I sigh in relief. I check on the youngest next. He's asleep.

I tell my boys to wake up. I beg them. I yell. I scream. I shake them. It doesn't feel real as I cry over them. I know they're alive, but they won't wake up. Why can't I wake them up? My boys, my joy, my happiness, please wake up for me!

I grab my youngest and I hold him in my arms. I run my fingers through his hair. My favorite. The youngest. My baby. I can't let him go. I beg him more and more to wake up. I look at his eyes—and they're painted!

I jump and throw my baby boy. My youngest child has become the doll! This can't be real! This can't be real! This can't be real!

The doll looks at me, his eyes of paint focused on my eyes. How did I let this happen? How could I let my joy become my pain? How could this be? My favorite—now the doll? Or did this make my boy the demon that lived inside the doll? Did I just see the demon's face? No, my boy cannot be either one! I see through the doll's lies. The doll wants to confuse me!

I look back to my other boys, and they're gone. No longer on the ground. Where have they gone? Where are my boys now? I call their names and I'm answered by nothing. I look back to where the doll had been, and now the doll is awake. He opens his mouth to speak.

I break down; I beg him to let them go—

Miranda woke up and immediately was struck with panic. She studied the doll, still in that ever-untouched place across the room. She fears for the boys' lives. Had the dream been real? Maybe it did happen.

She yelled for the boys to come to her, and they did. They sat by their mother on the bed and tried to calm her. Miranda wept. The boys were confused, but everything was all right in their house... until nighttime came again, and Miranda had her next dream.

***

Everything is upside down—my bed, my room, my house, my mind, my life. I'm the only thing right side up and—wait, where is the doll?

I look around. I can't find the doll. I step outside my room. I must find my boys.

I can run somehow. I can run on the upside-down stairs like it's no problem at all. I run into the youngest boy's room, the room where they were all asleep last time...

...and I'm right. I find them. My boys. On the ceiling. All on the ceiling. Or is it the floor? They're above me. I cannot reach them. I call them to get down. They look at me with their sick, upside-down eyes. Then I notice how even the smallest details are upside down and reversed—like my breaths, coming inside out.

I see the doll on the ground. His face is on upside down. The painted eyes, the thread for a mouth—his face is on upside down, and his eyes follow me as I step closer. He calls me. What does he want from me? What does he want from me? What does he want from me? Why does he do this to me?

My heart nearly stops dead. I'm suspended in place. The doll gets to his feet and raises his hands. I notice that his hands are upside down. I look back towards to ceiling in time to see my youngest fall to me. I catch him. I hold him. I hug him. He disappears. He's gone. I cry and I beg to get my son back, but the doll doesn't do anything—he just stands. My youngest boy is gone and I can't get him back.

My cries end when the middle child falls, except he falls through my hands. I have no chance to hold my boy. He falls through the ground, farther and farther. I can no longer see him, but I know he falls farther away every second. There's no telling how far he'll be.

My last hope is when my oldest boy falls to me. I catch him. The house starts to shift back. The upside-down shadow that possessed my dream is still draped over everything, but little by little things are moving back to normal. I'm still standing in an upside-down world, but at least a couple things are returning to normal.

I look back down at my son after I feel something. He's shrunk. For a second I think I am holding my youngest because he's so small now. He's shrinking. Fading away. I cry for him to not fade away, but he does. He fades like everything else in life. Suddenly, the few right-side-up things are now back to upside down, but it is worse now.

Now I can't un-see it—every detail sticking out and speaking to me. It's like a panic attack for my eyes. Every detail wants to be noticed. Every screw in a chair, every knob on a dresser, every fiber in the rug, every ring in the wood, every button on a shirt, every dent in a wall, every mark on my kids' spare shoes, and every paint stroke on the doll's face—it's all upside down and screaming to me to notice it.

***

Miranda awoke. She couldn't move at first. It took several minutes before she could. She fell in and out of sleep for hours. She felt miserable, trapped beneath the covers that clung to her skin. She was soaked with sweat.

It took a lot but she pushed past the covers. She sat up and saw the most horrific sight imaginable: The doll was upside down. The head was on the ground, and his stuffed feet were pointed towards the ceiling.

"Boys?" Her voice trembled, then it turned into a rage: "*Boys?* Where *are* you?"

The boys came running into their mother's room. Their faces were pale from fright, but Miranda did not notice or care.

"Who did it?" she asked calmly, then repeated herself when no one spoke up.

"Did—did what?" asked the oldest one.

"Don't act dumb!"

"Mommy, please," the youngest boy cried. The rest of his words were lost in sobs.

"The doll!" Miranda said. "Who moved the doll? Who touched it?"

The boys hadn't noticed that their mother's doll was touched. They looked towards it but the doll was no longer overturned. It was right side up. It was normal, not a fiber out of place. The smile on the doll seemed to know something.

"Mom, the doll is fine!" the oldest said.

"What?" Miranda turned to the doll.

The doll was fine. Maybe her son was right, maybe this was something that couldn't be fixed because maybe Miranda was just crazy. Maybe this was her only purpose in life, her destiny. Perhaps her sole purpose of living was to be a crazy woman and hallucinate about the stuffed doll that was supposedly filled with a demon.

***

The next night, a dream followed her.

The emptiness is filling me. I fall into the pit, and the walls close in on me. The falling doesn't stop, and neither does the pressing in of the walls. They press until I break into pieces... but the pieces are

45

still alive, falling further away. I feel the pain of every single piece, no matter how far they stray. The pit walls close in, and I'm left paper thin. The pieces become pieces. Pieces of pieces of me, all falling further down. I'm falling forever.

I become used to the falling. I know it's always there. I'm used to the sickening feeling, but I want it to disappear. I can't stop the falling, or the pressure from the closing walls; I'm as powerless as can be. I just wanna be safe. I just want my boys. I want the doll to leave me alone. I fear about what may wait for me at the end.

Some of my pieces reconnect, and the wall releases part of its grasp. The falling halts. As my pieces reattach, I see where I've landed; it's all darkness. I'm whole in the darkness, but the walls are still too tight against me. My neck is cramped and crooked.

What was I falling through this whole time?

Then I feel rain. It's back again. The demon inside the doll brought the rain back to me! And between the drops I can see glimpses of shimmering light that spreads out in gentle waves that shine down upon my skin. It illuminates the face of the doll.

I try to move but it all starts again. More pressure, more falling. Pieces turn into smaller pieces, and I feel every part of them splitting and falling. The atoms that make up my flesh tear into two and fall into microscopic universes, where they fall forever and ever. And the blood from my body spills across the walls and dwindles down into the emptiness.

Then I feel... then I feel...

Good.

Miranda woke up and felt great. Refreshed. It was a new day. A beautiful day. The sunshine came softly between her curtains, and it felt dazzling across her skin. She moved towards the curtains and opened them wide.

She saw the moon in the sky even though it was daytime. This made her happy.

When she turned her back to the window, the doll was gone. Who touched it?

Well, the boys must've moved it, she thought.

She wasn't mad. Oddly enough, she felt okay about it. She walked out of her room, up the stairs, and to the oldest boy's room.

Her hand knocked on the door, but she got no reply. She had a flashback to her dream but brushed it off. It was only a dream. She entered the room. No one was there. Slight panic rose in her shaking hands.

She barged into the middle child's room. No one.

She breathed heavily.

Oh Lord don't let anything be wrong with them, don't let a single hair on my precious boys' heads be out of place, please oh God let them be okay let them be okay!

Her hands shook as they both clasped over the golden knob to the youngest's room. She couldn't keep calm. She flung the door open to find her boys sleeping peacefully. She wiped the sweat off her forehead, relieved, and not knowing that her boys were dead.

STORY FIVE:

IF I DIE

If I die in my sleep, I hope I drift off into a flying dream. If I die in my sleep, I hope to soar through the calming airs into the seashell-shaped constellations filled with cosmic dots that overlap one another; I hope to jump through every single spot.

If I die in my sleep, I hope I drift off into a sinking dream. If I die in my sleep, I hope to propel myself to the depths of the blank ocean. If I die in my sleep, I hope to retain my senses to experience the bottom of the ocean in the way no living person can—feeling the current of waves pass over me in total darkness, just me and the sea.

If I die in my sleep, I hope I drift into an underground dream. If I die in my sleep, I hope to dig to the earth's core, and see the wonders of the unknown center of our world. If I die in my sleep, I hope to see every untold story in the earth's crust that was buried and lost like a forgotten dream.

If I die in my sleep, I hope to drift off into an invisible dream. If I die in my sleep, I hope to live inside the air. If I die in my sleep, I hope to drift around the entirety of existence—to spin freely in the ever-flowing stream of constantly expanding waves of energy.

If I die in my sleep, I hope to drift off into a storm. If I die in my sleep, I hope to be every droplet of rain that spills across the heavens. If I die in my sleep, I hope to be the calming presence that surrounds the storm.

If I die in my sleep, I hope to drift off into a pair of alluring eyes. Olive eyes. If I die in my sleep—oh, I can see it now—searching them deeper and deeper in my sleep, traveling them farther than I hope to travel the stars.

If I die in my sleep, I hope to drift off into the blue light that drifts across a forest. If I die in my sleep, I hope to slip into the mystifying, silent beauty that screams through the trees.

If I die in my sleep, I hope to drift off into the nightmare world. If I die in my sleep, I hope to see every hellish vision that a dream could give. If I die in my sleep, I hope to fathom all the haunting visions and voices that fill everyone's night terrors.

STORY SIX:

TRUE HAPPINESS

A girl walks through the Redwick forest beneath the soft silence that screams through the treetops. The cold air dries her running tears as another wave of air drags her sorrows around the forest. Her sadness is too much for her to bear.

"Crying," a voice from nowhere said. "It shows you feel. What're you feeling?"

"Huh?" The startled girl turned around. "Who said that?"

"I'm the watcher," replied the gruff voice.

"Where are you?" she asked through sniffles, still looking around.

"Watching," it answered. "Now, won't you tell me what's wrong?"

"I'm miserable."

"Why is that?"

"I'm lonely. Nobody loves me. Nobody will ever love me."

"How do you figure?"

"I'm ugly, I don't have a nice body, my voice isn't pretty."

"You should probably include snobby."

"Thanks, jerk. You sound just like everybody else."

"But I'm not like everybody else—not even close. I can change anything you want to change."

"Huh?"

"You can think of me as a genie. I can give you three wishes, and I don't even ask anything in return."

"Yeah, yeah. I already know how this goes. You're gonna screw me over. Everything backfires, or I somehow end up regretting what I wanted. You're just dying to already have me come crawling back to you to reverse everything. I don't buy it."

"I guarantee you, that couldn't be further from what'll happen."

"Okay, let's try it out then. I wish I were pretty."

"Okay, it's granted. When you walk back into town, you'll be the most beautiful girl in the state... however, I still think you're already the snobbiest."

"I wish I were rich, too. I don't need billions; let's just call it twenty—no! Thirty million."

"Sure thing. When you walk into town, it'll appear in your bank account. And legally, too. I assure you, there's nothing that'll backfire."

"All right! And to make sure of that, I use my last wish to make sure that none of my wishes backfire on me. That's my wish—that nothing I've wished for backfires."

"It is granted."

"I do have a question though."

"Shoot."

"Don't you ever have any desires? Do you ever use these wishes on yourself?"

"No, I never use any for myself."

"Why not?"

"I already have my purpose in life."

"What is it?"

"To distract people from snatchers."

STORY SEVEN:

ENDLESS KISSES

The hands on the clock across room pointed to just shy of 2 AM, but the darkness that wrapped around the room prevented Terry Kremer from seeing it. He counted sheep and stared into the abyss of a ceiling. His wife Holly slept next to him, her messy hair all over his arm. He had woken up out of the blue only minutes ago, but it felt like longer and sleep couldn't be any further from his mind.

Holly shifted towards him, her fingers intertwining with his and her elegant body rubbing against him. She laid her head on his shoulder and random strands of hair tickled his neck. He wrapped his arms around her.

"Didn't know you were up too," he told her. "I just woke up."

"Kiss me," she replied, running her fingers along his chest.

"What?" he asked. "I'm so tired, can we wait for morning?"

"Kiss me," she insisted.

He leaned over and kissed her lips, then moved back to lying down and staring towards the ceiling, feeling the warmth of her breath hitting him.

"Kiss me," Holly said again.

Terry reached over again and kissed her, then got comfortable again.

"Kiss me," she wouldn't stop saying. "Kiss me, kiss me, kiss me."

"Why do you want all these kisses?"

"Just kiss me." She slid on top of her husband.

She kissed him, but then he pulled away. His hand fumbled for the light switch above the bed, then turned it on. Holly's eyes were dull and lifeless as they rolled in their sockets. Her glassy smile was gone. Sickly cold replaced all the warmth in her body; she was as freezing as October winds. A slash along her neck dripped blood onto Terry's chest.

"Kiss me," a voice said from under the bed.

STORY EIGHT:

IF ONLY I REMEMBERED

I look up and see a single ray of light cutting through the darkness and to the top of a girl's face—all color leached from her eyes, and her straightened hair neatly placed above both shoulders while her head nods down. Although the darkness is powerful where I am, but I can still see the hazy form of her body. Her arms dangle, and her locked knees are frozen in place.

Something pokes at the back of both of my hands, but I can't see them like I see the girl. Despite my curiosity, I can't bring my hands to move. I'm not in control of them. I can feel them limp and dead at my sides; there's no life left in them.

"Who are we?" I ask her, my voice coming to little more than a whisper. It seems my eyes and jaw are all that can move. "Where are we? I'm afraid I don't remember."

She doesn't reply and I can't tell if she's silent because she's ignoring me, or because she can't move her mouth.

She must be like me, just frozen here in place. Weird that I can talk and she can't.

There's a cluster of voices coming from far off; their words and tones almost all acting in unison. There seems to be something distorting the noise, however, like how a napkin or plastic wrap around a speaker would muffle the noise.

A quick flash of light passes by the rest of her face and I'm able to glimpse what she looks like. What sticks out most is how her jaw is hanging open. I couldn't tell beforehand. And she's got these perfect cuts on both ends of her lips that go straight down her jaw. I wish I could've seen more.

The longer I wait here, the more I hear annoying hazes of noise flutter into my ears. If only I could hear them more clearly. If only I could remember myself. I *need* to remember the girl across from me. If only, if only, if only.

Footsteps reach closer to me. I can hear these perfectly clearly—they don't have anything muffling the noise. And suddenly, once the footsteps are right on top of me, I feel those things that were poking the back of my hands are moving.

My hands lift, my neck straightens out, and my legs are moving—all against my will. I was lifted up out of a box and pulled by my strings. I and the girl were nothing more than marionettes being used in a play.

STORY NINE:

THE WALLPAPER

A dim twilight draped over the town of Happiness, Arizona. The air was surprisingly cool for the time of year. The nature of the place was beautiful and bright; the name fit the place well. It's gonna be a big transition from the town I grew up in, a town called Carpenter.

Carpenter always felt gloomy and sad, even on the bright days when precious golden sunshine was abundant. There was something about the place that was unsettling. It took people a long time to realize this, and that was for those who *did* notice. It was unnerving to watch people whose whole lives went by without noticing something was amiss.

But that was in Carpenter, and now I am in Happiness. My husband, Collin, and I were finishing up the rest of the move into our first house. Collin paints full time. I, on the other hand, sculpt figures out of clay. It's a fun job and I don't think there's anything else on the earth that'd give me a bigger sense of accomplishment.

"Kavelle," Collin said from upstairs.

"Yes?" I said, walking up the wooden stairs.

He didn't reply. I found him in the first room on the right, staring at the walls.

"Yes?" I repeated myself.

"I think we're gonna have fun with this." He laughed and peeled a strand of wallpaper. "We get to peel it all off."

It was the only ugly room in the house. The once-white backgrounds on the wallpaper turned to an ugly cream and smelled old and musty, like the pages from a decades-old paperback book; thorny roses dancing in sporadic patterns were the main design on it, with the very bottom an image of water flowing steadily.

I briefly traced a rose with my finger then looked back to Collin.

"You're right, we are gonna have so much fun peeling the room top to bottom… have you thought about what you've wanted to put in here?"

"Probably just use it as a storage room."

"Fair enough."

I started to peel a strand and became transfixed by how oddly satisfying it felt. I looked back to Collin but he had left the room.

"Collin?" I called, but nobody replied.

I went down the steps and found Collin putting away clothes in our new bedroom.

"Collin?" I said again.

"Yes, my love?"

"Nothing, I…" my head felt heavy and dizziness made my eyes waver, "I just didn't realize you had left the room."

"I told you I was heading down here to put away our stuff before we get started on other rooms."

"Oh… I must not have heard you, then."

I turned around and went back up to the room of ugly wallpaper. Walking into that room was like walking into a bubble—in a good way. I could feel the air tightly wrap around me, but it wasn't bad at all—it was pleasing.

In the corner of the room, I started to peel the wallpaper. It came apart in annoying bits, and I knew I needed to buy a scraper and maybe some solvent to make it easier, but I was having fun. I peeled a long strand that reminded me of unwinding a Fruit by The Foot.

The next piece that I started to pull only went down an inch before a wave of colors ran across my eyes, the kind that overtake your vision when you stand up too fast. I blinked a couple times but kept on pulling and peeling. Oh, the joy of it, the joy of the peel. I couldn't stop peeling. I started to have a competition with myself to see how long of a piece I could get before it would snap off the wall.

I was hypnotized by the pattern of roses and thorns, watching them intertwine—they almost moved before my eyes, dancing and weaving and bobbing and twisting and… calling. Calling me. And I followed them around with my eyes and fingers, seeing how they all connected between the walls despite the large sections already torn off.

A real thorn poked me from the wall, and I watched a drop of blood hit the floor. I licked the blood from my finger and peeled the paper off from around that thorn, but all I could find around the thorn was solid wall. I pulled on the thorn and it came loose, but when I looked for it, it was gone, and all I saw was a strand of wallpaper connected from the wall to the tip of my left pointer finger; the paper had fused with my skin.

Confused, I pulled apart the paper that had connected to me. Some of my skin went with it and there was no pain. I looked around the room and noticed for the first time that I had peeled all the walls clean somehow. Was that real? I could've sworn I had so much more to do… but there I was seeing it with my own eyes.

I felt the sensation of peeling squirm and wiggle through the skin of my hands. I looked at my hand, bewitched by the feeling. I took my right pointer finger and thumb and grabbed a loose piece of skin atop my middle finger, just like I had grabbed the loose piece of wallpaper. I pulled it to the base of my fingers and studied the tear. The blood passionately slithered down my palm.

Now the tear of skin was at my wrist, and I wiggled my fingers to see the intricate systems I had exposed. I could see a vein swell and shrink, shrink and swell. I looked away from the vein to pull my skin down even more, but this time I yanked it a little to the left. The skin didn't snap. It moved freely along with my movements and it curled around the back of my wrist. I turned my arm around and pulled the skin down the back of my arm. The strand thinned as it went down, then it snapped off at my elbow.

I undressed the skin of my fingers by biting off a thin slice of skin with my teeth so I could have something to tug on. It didn't take much of a pull, and I was already past the wrist without giving it much of a thought. The urge to peel kept growing.

The next strand I tore got halfway between my elbow and shoulder before it snapped, and as it did, the urge to peel reverberated throughout my entire being, and I was enthralled with the idea of peeling more of myself.

I looked down at the walls and noticed real thorns started to grow out of the water design on the wallpaper bottoms. I took off my clothes and set them in a pile in the middle of the room. I stared at the thorn then placed each of my fingers on their own personal thorn. I dug the thorns clean through my fingers. I loved it.

I started to explore the thorns by rubbing my arms across them, and soon the skin on my arms looked just like the wallpaper did when the hard to peel spots were left on the wall and I needed wallpaper remover and a scraper.

I desired to peel the rest of me. I craved it—there was nothing I desired more. I slowly placed my chest on the thorns and they dug into my breasts and pulled out chunks of flesh. My skin was tickled by the sudden warmness that washed upon me.

I dug my finger into the skin on the bottom of my breast and pulled back most of the skin. It tore clean off around my armpit. I noticed the smallest scratch in the middle of my chest. It wasn't big enough to count as a cut, but it would do.

My finger found a home inside the scratch, and the scratch turned into a waterfall of blood. I put another finger inside and pulled down with both of them. My skin exploded open with the biggest tear of them all by the time I reached the end of my ribs.

I collapsed and found it hard to move in the mess of blood and insides that I was on top of. I reached for the thorns, I needed to grasp them. I needed to be poked by them, I needed to peel myself. I reached for them, but they seemed so far out of my reach.

I felt mocked by the thorns. They stared back at me. My eyes drifted to the water design that now looked beautiful. I focused on the water, it was all I could do... then I felt the waves, the beautiful, cooling waves splashing against me.

STORY TEN:

DEEP SLEEP

The sun's reflection filled the lake in East Oxide, and its warmth filled the air around it. Along the shore sat a house that belonged to man named Mason Neil. Swimming made him happy, and on this morning he was outside and ready to jump into the lake.

He was submerged in the beautiful, clear waters. He came up from the warmth of the waves, then an odd feeling—an emptiness—took hold of him. It was something he couldn't shake; his insides shifted and he almost threw up.

He looked around. Everything surrounding the lake felt like a cheap imitation of its true self. The birds did not chirp, the waves were not moving, and the sky felt like a painting. He looked down at the water and even it felt fake, as though he was torn from existence and placed inside a book.

The feeling pounded at his brain as he left the water.
What could it be?

It got worse by the time he got to the doorway of his house. He looked back to the dreadful sky and saw the moon—even though it was day—hiding behind a thin cloud.

Why do I feel like I should know what this is?

His house still had feelings of normality but it could not soothe his troubled mind. He took a shower, hoping that the scalding water would burn away these ugly feelings that crawled deeper into his body, but no amount of burning could get rid of it. His whole life had become a cheap copy of the original; the wood paneling on the walls did not shine the way it should, and the recently washed windows suddenly were filled with grime.

No amount of sleep could make it go away, either. Even sleep was different—it seemed like it didn't exist; suddenly mankind wasn't made to sleep, we were made to always be awake, even when tired. He stared at the floor next to his bed, staring into the same spot until the complete darkness in his vision swirled into a vast nothingness. His body shook with a shiver as he felt that maybe he'd fall into this void and disappear forever.

The moon hadn't moved in the sky, even though he had counted a thousand sheep and then counted the dust motes floating on the moonbeam. He rolled one way and then another. That was his night for hours on top of hours. He wasn't sure when it happened, but his eyes finally shut enough to sleep. It was only for a couple hours, but it was nice. Sleep was the only thing that didn't feel like a mockery.

The moment his eyes cracked open, he knew the feeling was still there. The sense of oddness pestered his mind; it trailed his every thought and settled around his spirit, across his body, and inside his hands. The feeling kept growing. It pulsed throughout his body like it was going to take over his heartbeat and burst his body open.

But if there was one person he could talk to about it, it would be his friend Joshua.

Manon eased his car down the road. Parked cars lined the street, but no one else drove. At first he didn't notice, but by the time he reached the last light before he got to Joshua's house, he realized how alone he was. Nervousness grew in his stomach. He needed to see another person.

He sped through the red light then parked in front of Joshua's. Worry grew in tandem with the odd feeling that hit like a sledgehammer against his skull. The knob felt so damn cold as it touched his fingertips. He pulled away for a moment, stared at the knob, then grabbed it again and turned it.

He stepped into the kitchen. Joshua and his girlfriend, Courtney, slouched over the table, their heads plopped into the food they had been eating. Mason ran to them and moved their faces out of the dishes. Their eyes were still wide open.

"Josh? Courtney?" He shook them, then screamed. Neither one gave a reply, and neither one had a pulse.

He screamed so loudly it hurt his throat. He felt bad for leaving them. His knees wobbled and his hands shook, making it difficult to open the car door, start it, and drive away, but he managed. It wasn't so bad driving wild with no other cars to look out for.

The air seemed to thin around him. Breathing was difficult; his lungs felt as if water had filled them and there was no longer room for air. A rising panic came upon him, and his mind spun and his face flooded with heat. The odd feeling had him in its grasp and there was no way in hell it was going to let go.

He parked the car at the police station and jumped out without shutting the car door behind him. It was hard to focus because the earth below him felt like he was running on top of jelly and he would probably tumble over at any second; the thickness of the ground sucked at his feet like swamp mud. He grasped the wall of the building and tried not to fall over. His head was going to burst.

Need to do this...

He pushed through the dizziness—as tough as it was—and held the door handle. He looked to his reflection in the glass doors and its eyes held his.

"What is going on?" he said to the reflection, sounding so certain that it would reply.

Mason Neil took a big breath then forced the door open. It felt as heavy as a house. Every single person in the building was slouched over just as Josh and Courtney had been.

His thoughts couldn't keep up with his actions. Suddenly his legs had strength again and he walked over to every person he could find. It was as if God had snapped his fingers and everyone but Mason Neil fell dead. There were no wounds from a knife or gunshot, or any markings at all. Not even the slightest sign of a struggle. Everyone lay peacefully dead.

The odd feeling struck him so immensely that he felt it popping out of him and into the very air that he breathed. He left the police station, no longer dizzy. There was no use reentering the car. He walked to the closest house. The door was locked so he grabbed a large stone from the garden in the backyard and broke off the knob. Upon entering the house, a layer of realization settled upon his mind. He saw an old lady and an old man plopped over on the floor.

Mason Neil was the only man left.

He fell to his knees, but tears would not escape. Somehow, it didn't feel real enough for tears. Everything was as fake as the paper moon in the sky. He crawled out of the home he was in, then lay down on the lawn.

He stared to the sky in hope of answers but there wasn't a snowball's chance in hell that he'd get any. Slowly, without taking his eyes off the sky, he got back to his feet and reentered the house he had broken into.

On his right side was the sink and dishrack. The set of knives next to them called his name. He grabbed the smallest one and held it to his wrist as lightly as holding a small brush to a canvas. His hand didn't tremble as it moved the knife. He moved it too lightly to even scratch himself. Deep down, he wanted this, yet deep down he felt regret.

As he pushed down harder, a voice said, "Mason…"

Mason turned around, at first thinking maybe it was the dead man, then realizing it was not.

"Yes? Hello? I'm here!" Mason said, waiting for a reply. Then, after a moment of silence: "Hello? Who's there? Where are you?"

Excitement bloomed inside of him as he walked to the door, hoping to find someone waiting for him, someone who could explain this hellhole he fell into.

The voice called again. The odd feeling began to fade. Joy shot through his body. He was glad to hear a voice that wasn't his own.

"Yes! I'm Mason!" He ran down the steps of the house. "Who are you? Where are you?"

"Mason?" The voice became a sob, then a cry.

Mason chased after the sound of the voice, but it faded. The more he chased, the less he heard. Somebody knew who he was, somebody knew what was going on, somebody had answers—but he just couldn't find them.

The odd feeling regrew as the cry vanished.

"Come back!" Mason screamed to the sky and ran down the street. "I'm here! I'm Mason! Someone please answer me!"

But the voice was completely gone. Nobody was calling him; there were no sounds, and Mason was left standing in a world devoid of noises. Mason was all alone in the world of death—loneliness was the only thing that wouldn't leave him.

His feet turned heavy again and the odd feeling was popping back into his mind. He wished so badly to scream, thinking maybe that would make the feeling stop, but he had yelled enough today and his screaming would do him no good. He walked back to his car, tears flowing and his mind scrambled. He checked his mirrors and stopped at all the stop signs although he knew it was useless. He craved normality in a place where nothing was normal.

He drank whiskey until he fell asleep—and tonight, the sleep felt normal. But in the morning he was greeted by a cry—nearly inaudible at first, then growing into a terrible screech.

"Who's crying? Who's there?" Mason said. "Listen to me—are you all right?"

Mason ran through his house trying to find the crying voice, but there was nobody there.

"Please come out!" he said.

He heard the voice crying from inside the wall next to him. He put his ear to and the coldness send a chill through his head.

"Hello? Are you in there?"

The cries sounded like they were coming from another world—then they faded. The odd feeling would not stop growing—it overtook his sanity. He could feel it flowing through his blood and into his heart.

***

That first year of loneliness was the worst. There was crying every day. The voice multiplied into multiple voices, and they never seemed to end. The bodies never seemed to change—no one had decayed, their hair and nails never grew. Everyone was frozen in time.

Five years passed—and quickly. The odd feeling never left him. It kept him company. Mason pretended the outside world was normal and rarely left his house. It was a difficult adjustment but he felt no greater pain than seeing everyone paused in existence. The odd feeling was all he had left in life. The strange voices still bugged him.

I need to know! I need to know! Did everybody's soul leave to heaven? Are these voices just people calling me from the afterlife, trying to tell me ta join them?

The mysterious cries kept knocking at his brain. He could never understand where they came from or who they even were.

***

Only six months had passed since the accident. Mason died in the hospital bed, surrounded by his loved ones. He would've drowned that morning if Joshua never found him. But now the coma was over, and Mason would no longer hear any mourning or crying.

STORY ELEVEN:

IMAGINATION

"Rose," Corinne said to her little sister, as she sat on the edge of bed, "I want to talk to you about something."

"What? I'm tired, I wanna sleep," Rose replied.

"It's best I tell you now. I should've told you earlier…"

Rose shifted her small body, then sat up. Her eyes caught the seriousness of Corinne's eyes, then she said, "Is it that serious?"

"Yeah, Rosie… it is." Corinne took a deep breath, then continued: "What if I told you that your whole entire life was nothing more than a dream within a dream?"

A confused "Huh?" was all Rose could think to say.

"I want you to listen to me, and listen to me good—"

"Then you shouldn't talk to me when I'm so tired, Corinne."

"I'm sorry," Corinne said, "but this is important and I couldn't wait any longer, okay?"

"Okay, then go on with it."

"Rose, do you know where you come from?"

"I'm old enough to know where babies come from, I'm fourteen."

"Yeah, but... you were born a long time ago, you're older than fourteen. You're even older than me."

"Come on, if you were gonna try making a joke you could've at least made it funny." Rose rolled her eyes.

"You're a brain in a jar is what you are," Corinne rubbed her eyes. "Your brain was kept because when you were alive, you enrolled in a government program to test whether or not consciousness could be digitalized— which, In this day and age, everything is. And there was going to be—well, there is... there is testing to see if it was possible."

"I've lived my whole life in this house with you and mom and dad and our cat. I'm not a brain in a jar... you don't even sound like a person right now. Look—" Rose placed her hand on Corinne's arm, "you can feel me. You can feel my hand and the heat coming from it. I can feel your arm and the little hairs on it... you need to do something about that... but you can't digitalize a feeling. You can't digitalize heat and emotions."

"I can go into detail if you want, about how it's all possible."

"Fine. Whatever. You woke me up anyway, might as well let you waste more of my time."

"Your brain is forty-six years old. When your body was thirty-two, it was brought into a lab. You had died from an infection from an animal bite. Your brain was placed into a holding chamber, where we have it now submerged in a liquid called Neprine, which preserves it."

"Okay."

"Twelve years ago, they started feeding your brain data, various scenarios. They—"

"Your story already is messed up with plot holes. Where's my consciousness? None of this would've been me. *If* you're feeding me new thoughts and scenarios, you're making a totally new person."

"Oh, no, Rosie. This is exactly what they tried to do. They wanted to ease you in with the idea of being a downloaded consciousness before they—"

"This isn't easing at all. This doesn't make sense. That's not easing, that's dumping a whole load on someone… a whole load of shit. Can you get out my room now, please?"

Corinne got up and left without a word, and an annoyed Rose tried to fall back asleep, but couldn't. It wasn't that she believed the outrageous claims of her sister, it was the mere fact that it might be possible, no matter how many times Corinne seemed to contradict herself.

Rose supposed she could be just a brain in a jar. After all, we are all just brains operating meat suits… but could she seriously only be a brain living in a jar, with fake memories fed to her? Could she just be a—a digital mind?

It couldn't be true. Rose traced over the scar on her hip, the scar from a cut she got when another kid tripped over her at recess when she was in the third grade. The scar had stuck with her for years, and it sure felt and looked real. But couldn't a planted memory feel and look just as real? If it were simply planted there, then of course she'd think it were real…

Could a memory be planted? Well if anything she said were true, I mean, I guess that would explain the forgotten memories throughout my life. The blank spots I don't remember. Especially when I was like, eight or nine... but does anybody really remember much from that age?

The thought of not being able to recall every memory terrified her. What happened in all those blank spots? She could remember certain spots in childhood, she could remember certain spots going back a year or two, but the missing parts... well, she didn't like thinking what the missing parts could mean.

Digital memories... was it possible? Could we really have come that far? I mean, suddenly this makes sense. If I am a brain in a jar I guess this would be the way of easing me into understanding it. Is Corinne right?

I think they knew I wouldn't believe it. That could be their plan. Then after time goes by and the idea gets more believable then suddenly it wouldn't be such a dramatic thought.... Either Corinne is trying to freak me out or she's telling the truth.

Rose felt her face. She coughed just to cough and blinked just to blink. She wiggled her toes just to wiggle her toes, then thought about how silly she was being. She could move, and movements weren't thoughts. Movements couldn't be digitalized, movements were just movements. Rose was Rose, and that's all she was. That's all she could be.

Regardless of anything she tried telling herself, the subtle hint of possibility and belief lingered. It could be true, and she'd have no way of knowing for sure. That was the scariest part. Corinne could be right, Corinne could've been telling her the truth—and maybe she just tossed that truth out the window. But Corinne could've also been joking…

What am I supposed to believe? Oh, I sound foolish. And all the random people I've passed by in life, driven past, or whatever… were they just lifeless background characters or did they have life? How would you program hundreds of thousands of different background people? What would've happened if I talked to one? Would they not react, simply because they were a digital program, and only programmed to stand there? Or would they reply? Were they… programmed to reply? Did they have a whole life implanted in their brains, or did they have automated responses plugged into them? Oh gosh, I'm sounding like I believe Corinne.

And why should I believe Corinne? We have the typical love-hate sisterly friendship. If they programmed that, then it seems lazy and unoriginal. And if these memories are all planted, was my interaction with Corinne just planted? Could she just be a floating brain too? Could she be the one imagining this and I'm the side character? Could these very thoughts just be numbers on a screen, transmitted from one computer to another and into her mind? All uploaded and studied by scientists?

Get a grip on yourself, Rose. You can't believe your annoying older sister. That's what an older sister's job is, isn't it? To be annoying. Speaking from experience, that's what Corinne has been most of your life. But what if this is the one time she wasn't trying to be annoying? What if she was being genuine? Can I throw that out the window? But how can I believe it?

Seriously, Rose, how long have you spent awake right now just because Corinne told you one stupid joke? This is stupid. Don't stoop to Corinne's level. She's a jerk, you already know this. You don't have to wiggle your toes all night just to know and believe you're more than a brain. You are more than a brain, you're you, nobody else could be you, and that's beautiful... but everyone can be just a brain in a jar with fake memories, so am I that? Am I Rose the person, or am I Rose the brain who's a test subject?

NO!

Rose, you are Rose! Corinne is Corinne. Mom is Mom, Dad is Dad, Alaska my cat is Alaska my cat, and a coffee cup of drain cleaner is a coffee cup of drain cleaner. I don't know what else I can tell you—what else I can tell myself. Maybe you could just talk to Corinne—

NO! Corinne would laugh at me and make fun of me... Corinne would never let me live this down. It'll be Thanksgiving dinner thirty years from now and she'll still be bringing it up. I can hear her now, 'Remember when you were twelve and you came to me crying in the middle of the night because you thought you didn't exist?'

Rose realized she was crying. Corinne got her good. Here she was late in the night, eyes filled with tears and mind filled with worry. What Corinne said wasn't scary at all, the thought wasn't scary, it was her imagination running wild with the idea, and believing it was what scared her.

Rose sat up and wiped the tears away. She looked around her dark room. She saw Alaska sleeping—and looking adorable—in her little bed next to Rose's. This couldn't have all been faked, could it? And what would happen once they placed the memory of dying in her? Was there any coming back from that memory?

She got out her bed and crept out the doorway. The threshold of darkness didn't faze her. Rose was alone with the natural sounds of her family's house. The thoughts in her head couldn't have gotten any sillier. She almost fell to the floor in a flood of laughs at the idea of this whole house being a programmed thought.

The stairs to the next floor of the house did not creak, and Rose thought that if this was all just a program, she was happy that they didn't think to program steps that creaked. She got to Corinne's door and turned the knob. She peeked her head into the room.

"Corinne?" Rose whispered "Are you awake?"

Rose heard a snore, that was answer enough. She walked to her sister and shook her.

"Corinne?"

Suddenly, the bed was empty, and the covers fell away from Rose's fingers. She looked around the room. Slowly, her memories of Corinne faded. She never knew a Corinne, and forgot why she entered the room in the first place.

Back in her room, Rose drifted off to sleep. Rose was happy.

***

Corinne's consciousness traveled down the digital waves of creation and was swept through tides of data and currents of information in a fraction of a second. Her mind and freedom were trapped again in her floating brain.

The fat finger of a scientist tapped the glass.

"Not so fast!" he laughed, "You almost got through to her, but I don't think she's ready for that.

The scientist sat back down in his seat and stared at the numbers that popped up as he typed.

"You're not telling Rose a single thing. I don't know how you clawed your way through the system, but I'm lucky I caught you, Miss Corinne. How were you able to do such a thing?"

He looked at the container as though he was looking at the eyes of a person.

"Placing false memories of your own inside of Rose's head. I wonder how you learned to do that. Is there someone in that tank teaching you, or did you learn from watching me? Regardless, I wonder how this will affect Rose's brain. I erased everything false that you gave her. She's back to knowing the life of an only child and her cat."

The scientist looked over at the container that had Rose's brain.

"Ah, Miss Rose. How much fun I'll have studying you and the others after this incident."

But for now, Rose was happy and asleep under covers that were programmed to be warm, in a house that programmed to be dark, in a world programmed to be just for her.

STORY TWELVE:

UNHEARD VOICES

Maybe it's been speaking to me this whole time—if I had only tried to listen.

Heavy rain spilled across the open fields between Redwick and Happiness. The trees quivered and whacked in the whistling winds of the night storm. The only car on the road on this particularly hot night was that of Jerry Nolan and his wife, Evelyn.

Evelyn's eyes naturally sparkled, like ice on a car window under a streetlight. Jerry's eyes were as dark as a shadow, with equally dark bags under them. Evelyn and Jerry were exhausted from the long drive. The vacation was fun, but they were glad to be headed home. The darkness of the sky dwindled down into the road ahead; it was nearly impossible to see through that on top of the thickening rains. Jerry pulled over to the side of the road. All was dark, not a thing was in sight—until the lightning broke across the heavens and its light illuminated a mansion that he had not seen in the moments previous. It seemed motionless and stood apart from the world.

The mansion was built more with size in mind than comfort and luxury; it looked plain—devoid of decorations. It stood three tall stories, spanning about seven—maybe more—rooms across each floor. On the right was the thick oak entrance door that overlooked a clear path of square stones which seemed to attract the rainwater like moths to a lamp.

The lightning flashed again, this time revealing through the ocean of rain and darkness another car parked ahead of them.

Jerry turned to his wife, "Should we go in?"

"I don't see what other choice we have." She said. "Either be cold in our car all night or see if they have room in that place. We've got cash, we can pay them."

***

The large Redwick table was probably the most beautiful thing in the front room. The table was separated into two sides, with blue glass joining them to appear as a lake suspended in time, caught flowing through a tree. The rounded edges had a hatching design carved in it.

Alycen Cochran and her twin sister Kristy had papers and junk spread out atop the pretty table. The only way to tell the ladies apart was by their hair—Kristy dyed hers brown and kept it up in a bun, Alycen kept her hair its natural blonde color and wore it down in curls.

Just days ago they inherited the family mansion they had seldom visited before. They weren't quite moved in yet and nobody knew they were here.

"This has not been my day," Kristy said. "So much more to unpack and many boxes to move around."

Alycen replied, "Yeah. Oh, and then tomorrow we—"

KNOCK! KNOCK! KNOCK!

Alycen jumped with fright from the unexpected knock and bumped into Kristy, who was also scared.

They gave each other a look before creeping to the door. First Alycen looked through the peephole, then Kristy did.

"I don't think we should," Alycen said.

Kristy rolled her eyes, "They're probably just stuck in the rain, open it."

And so Alycen did.

"Hello," the man said, "my wife and I were driving, but the rain is heavy and it's impossible to see in front of us tonight. Do you guys happen to have an extra—"

"We just moved in, and I don't think we have much to offer you, but we can at least keep you out of the rain for a bit." Kristy said, then moved to let them in.

There it is again.

Kristy led them to the long couch by the fireplace as Alycen grabbed them drinks.

"Where were you headed?" Kristy asked.

Alycen walked back into the room, "Hope water's okay, we didn't go shopping yet so we're all out of Ginger ale."

"Thank you," Evelyn said. She took a sip, then answered: "Coming back from a trip to New York. I'm Evelyn. This is my husband, Jerry."

"Well it's nice to meet you guys," said Alycen.

"Give it time." Jerry laughed. "And by the way, this place looks incredible."

"Thank you." Alycen said. "It's been in our family a long time... so long that I don't even know when it was built."

"1820 or so," Kristy said. "About 150 years, give or take."

"Interesting," Evelyn said. "And I don't mean to sound rude, but can you show us to a room, please? I'm awful cold and my eyes are tired."

The twins took their guests to the top floor and to the middle room, but stopped inside of the storage room at the end of the hall to look for sheets and pillows.

"So much extra stuff in here," Alycen said. "Great-grandpa was a packrat with a spendin' habit. Gambling habit, too. He was a moron and nearly lost it all—oh, why am I ranting? You don't care and I hardly knew him."

Even the junk in this room was better than the stuff Evelyn had grown up with. The wealth of this building astonished her—not that there was much glory in this room, it was mostly stuff that nobody had any use for anymore. Evelyn noticed a date carved into a lower panel of wood: April 9, 1961.

What are these voices pulsing in my head?

"What's this date?" Evelyn asked and traced it with her finger.

"Oh gosh, I forgot about that," Alycen walked towards the wall. "I—that feels like a whole lifetime ago. I did that the first time I came here because I noticed somebody carved a date a few feet down." she led Evelyn to the spot: "1889."

***

It didn't take long for Evelyn to fall asleep. Jerry wasn't so lucky; he tossed and turned but sleep escaped him every time he shut his eyes. He tried to move his body to a comfortable position, but was suddenly frozen—no part of him would move.

He struggled and found a little feeling in his hands, but not enough to get them to move. The grip over him drifted around his whole being. Everything was halted, even the rushing blood stayed in place. He couldn't even breathe.

The force that spread all around him lifted him upward. He levitated a few inches above the mattress. Terror was the only thing that wouldn't halt. Footsteps came from the hall. The pounding feet came closer and closer. He prayed it was one of the twins and that they'd know how to stop it. He prayed and prayed to anyone who would listen—to anyone who could hear. More panic raced through his mind. The sound of footsteps was next to him.

A stranger's hand touched Jerry's throat and commanded the force to let him go. Jerry looked to his savior but saw no one. A delayed scream left his throat as he shot up and with hands on his head. Evelyn nearly fell off the bed.

"Shit." She said. "Are you okay?" she could barely speak, her heart raced from the screams. "Did—did something scare you?"

"No, I just wanted to see if you were awake," he said. A shadow of fear played on his face.

His explanation was short. He took her by the hand and hurried down the stairs, worrying that the force would freeze him and send him tumbling down the staircase to his death. Evelyn was dazed.

On the bottom floor, Jerry saw the rains pouring outside a window. There was no sound at all coming from the world outside the walls. He let go of Evelyn's hand and put both of his on the door handles. Even using every ounce of the strength he had, he couldn't open the door—not even a budge. He tried for the windows in desperation, but even those seemed impossible to open.

He grabbed Kristy's paperweight off the table and struck the glass with all the force his arm could muster. The glass stayed still. The frustration and commotion woke Alycen and Kristy, who walked into the front room, hesitant and confused.

"Let us out!" Jerry shouted. "Out!"

"What's wrong?" Kristy asked. "Did something happen?"

"I can't explain it! It's as if something was in there with us and grabbing me!"

"And you—and you can't open the door?"

"It won't move."

Kristy tried the door. Jerry was right, it wouldn't open. Alycen took her turn, then even Evelyn tried, but nobody had any luck. The doors wouldn't move one iota. They all searched for exists as the soundless rains showered atop the house.

If I had only listened.

***

Jerry woke up in the late afternoon in front of the oak entrance door. There was a gloomy sense hovering over him. Evelyn was asleep next to him. He had no memories from most of the night. Alycen and Kristy never fell asleep; the exhausted ladies spent every hour of the night trying to find a way to leave the mansion.

If I had only...

Jerry woke up Evelyn then looked around for the sisters and found them in the kitchen looking through cabinets. The terrified four were on edge. A quick, powerful gust of wind knocked everyone to the ground.

"What the hell?" Jerry said.

If I had...

"Dammit, what is wrong with this house?" Jerry shouted. "What did you get us into?"

"What did we get you into?" Kristy said. "You're the one who stopped here."

If I...

"Oh, don't start an argument," Evelyn said, "it's not gonna help us solve anything."

A subtle creak caught everyone's attention. There in the doorway was a living corpse—the shriveled gray and green skin was torn across the scalp and down to empty eye sockets.

If...

Everyone dashed out of the kitchen with shrieks and cries. Jerry was the only one to go for the door, the ladies went for the stairs.

I don't know what I'll do if it opens and I leave without Evelyn, but that's a chance I'm willing to take.

It didn't open. He heard the ladies crying and calling from the stairway. The corpse appeared behind Jerry and gooey breath hit his neck. The force from earlier fell upon him. There was no way on earth that Jerry could move away from the corpse. The corpse placed both hands were placed on him; one on his neck, the other on his chest. *God, Satan, Buddha, whoever can hear me, I'm begging you, please—*

And as though someone had listened, the force stopping him was gone. Adrenalin kicked in as he pushed the corpse away, his hands tingling from the touch of rotting flesh, his stomach on the verge of throwing up whatever was in it from the godawful smell. His feet never ran faster than they had now. He shouted for Evelyn as he went up the stairs. She called to him.

The ladies were hiding in the storage room. They couldn't have shut the door behind Jerry fast enough.

"Oh God, oh God!" Alycen paced the room. "We're all gonna die."

Time passed. They each took turns holding an ear to the door, making sure nothing was coming their way, but uncertain what to do if it did. They worried if there'd be multiple corpses or just the one. Alycen was the most frantic of the bunch.

Alycen mumbled to herself in the corner of the room. Her thoughts were terrifying her more than the corpse was; horrible situations played over and over again in her mind. The room was filled with thousands of old items and possessions but the only thing that distracted her—even if it was just a moment's thought—was the doll she saw poking out of a box. *I know somebody who'd love that.*

"I think it's safe to say it isn't coming up here," Kristy said. "And it does us no good if we starve to death. I think if we... if we get to the roof, we can signal someone for help..."

"I agree," Jerry said.

"So do I," Evelyn nodded.

They had to repeat it for Alycen, but she agreed.

The thud of the lock made everyone nervous. The stairs to the roof were behind the door across from this room. Jerry held the door open for the women then went up the stairs himself, constantly checking behind his shoulder. The feeling of the corpse touching him would never leave his mind.

The roof was so dry it was as if it never rained in the first place. It was flat with three-foot high edges. They all faced the road. Jerry regretted ever leaving the car. He wished to be behind the wheel and driving away, never to see this place again.

Then the terrible moan of the corpse sounded from the doorway, and all four faces as pale as the moon turned to it and shrieked. It moaned again and stepped forward, arms outstretched and moving sloppily like a marionette.

There's only one way out of this.

Alycen Cochran jumped off the edge of the roof and plummeted to her death.

The others looked down to her splattered body upon the entrance to Cochran home. Alycen's mind had been troubled with strange thoughts of corpses, but to the others—to the others, it was a beautiful day with the warmth of the sun falling over them, and it was a perfect day for Jerry and Evelyn to get back on the road.

STORY THIRTEEN:

SEQUOIA' S DREAM

I was trapped in a disturbing dream; the noise of footsteps echoed all around the empty hallway. They sounded so… so vile, like the sinister clacking of a claw on tile. I followed them as closely as possible until I stumbled upon an energetic room that was as black as ink. I moved close to the footsteps—they were now coming from the corner of the room—and it seemed as though the inky color of the walls drifted into the air and crawled upon my eyes, blinding me.

Then suddenly, I was in the upstairs room despite never having left the dark room. I could see again—I was in my room, but it began to change its appearance—it was no longer the room I recognized. The door no longer existed. The windows disappeared, too. I was trapped.

Candle wax dripped down from the fan. Its candy-apple color shone in the silver light that drizzled down from the ceiling corners. Traces of a breeze wrapped around me. All I could hear was the *drip, drip, drip* of the wax hitting the floor.

A small suitcase fell from amid the wax. I looked upon the bobbing zipper and I'm worried. Something moved around inside of it, but my hand opened it before I could even think. I looked at the passageway and went into the unknown threshold that was before me. The inside was an entrance of beech tree stairs. They felt wonderful beneath my feet. Every step stunned me to the point where I couldn't breathe.

The surroundings in the suitcase were made up of trees of all varying in sizes, but each one scattered with blinking eyes in every direction. It puzzled me how anything could frighten me but be so beautiful.

The last step brought me to a room of walls made of plastic heads, and a floor and ceiling made of outstretched hands. It was as if a gumball machine of souls had broken loose. There was a small window set between a chubby plastic head with bright-blue eyes, and a small head with kiwi eyes and a chipped smile. The window overlooked a still river of decapitated bodies, restlessly swimming in unison inside a cellophane river that extended from nowhere to nowhere. A balloon passed overhead and grimly danced in the invisible motions of the swaying currents.

And then I woke up. Red wax dripped from the fan onto my bed.

STORY FOURTEEN:

THE DOCTOR WILL SEE YOU NOW

"The doctor will see you now." The silvery voice of a nurse called from down the hall.

I looked around but didn't see a nurse; in fact, I didn't see anyone. I was the only person among the empty chairs in the brightly lit room. I stood up and looked around just to be sure there wasn't a nurse, but I saw nobody.

I heard the voice, again coming from down the empty hall. I walked nearer to the voice and paused in front of the door that I was absolutely positive the voice was now coming from. Peering through the window, all I saw was a man—the doctor—facing away and looking at some papers on a table. I opened the door and walked inside.

"Excuse me," I said, "but I think the nurse was calling for me to see the doctor. Are you who I'm supposed to see?"

He turned around and stared at me. Large, scissor blades clipped against each other in his right hand. His vile and beady little eyes studied me. His hair was short and messy. Suddenly, his left hand—surprisingly stringy and soft—grabbed me and pushed me into a seat.

He dropped the scissors and used both hands to strap my arms to the chair. I tried to fight back, but he was too strong for me. He strapped my feet to the chair legs after he was done with my hands; I tried to kick but he held them down tight and I could feel the bruises emerging on my feet.

"Now, tell the doctor what is wrong," he said.

"Why did you strap me down?"

"We can't have you throwing more fits. Is that why you came in today? Is it the fits?"

"What fits?"

"Tell the doctor exactly what is wrong."

"Untie me. Nothing is wrong."

I really didn't know what was wrong. Why was I here? Come to think of it, I couldn't remember entering the building at all; it was like I was suddenly plopped here and this day was the first day of my existence.

But then I felt it. It was small—unnoticeable at first—but with every worry or bad thought I had here, it grew. It was swelling; an immeasurable pain, yet only the size of a water droplet. It was annoying, and it was in the middle of my throat. I wanted to rip my hands out from the straps and claw at my own throat. Was he right about the fits? Would this have been one of them?

"Doctor, my throat—" I almost couldn't breathe.

"Yes, okay. Your throat. What's the problem?"

"There's something in there! There's something in my throat! Take a look!"

I opened my mouth. He looked inside with a flashlight, then he felt around my neck with a cold metal tool.

"What's wrong with me, doctor?" I asked once he finished looking.

"As far as I can tell, there's nothing wrong with you. Not a single thing wrong," the doctor replied.

"But doctor, I can feel it!" I said, worried.

The worry only made it grow. The pain in my neck, the water droplet-sized thing that was in there, had grown.

"Doctor, it's getting worse." I cried, but still, that only made it feel worse.

The doctor wrote something down, then looked at my throat again.

"I can't find a single thing wrong."

"Doctor, cut it out if you have to, but something is in my throat."

I tried not to worry, but it grew, and I could feel the walls of my throat getting clogged up and my throat bulging. I was so damn scared and dizzy, and my head felt as though it was as heavy as a house. I was beyond terrified. I had no clue how to handle this.

I then felt air bubbles form around the pain that was in my throat. I tried to pop them like burps but it only made more come back. I could feel the air seep through the walls of my throat and form air bubbles in pockets under the very skin on my neck.

"*Doc-tor!*" I choked. "*Please!*"

The doctor looked at me like I was crazy. He looked around a cabinet for a moment then turned back to me.

"I have to get it from another room, I'll have the nurse keep you company."

The doctor opened the door and called for the nurse. Nobody came in, but apparently, the doctor thought somebody was there, because he spoke to the emptiness that accompanied us in the room and told it to keep watch over me.

I wiggled my arm and tried to free myself, but my muscles strained and all it did was hurt me. A flash of worry and fear deeper than I had ever fathomed ran through my heart and into my body, and my throat started to shake. If I were glass, my throat would've shattered into dust.

Before my very eyes, the straps undid themselves. They unlatched and pulled apart as if guided by gentle, invisible hands. Maybe somebody was watching me after all. I grabbed my throat and rubbed it. To my surprise, it felt normal to the touch—but I still felt the bubbles and stretched out walls on the inside, and as soon as my hands left my throat, I felt the pain twice over.

I undid the straps around my feet then stood up and grabbed the scissors the doctor had in his hand earlier. I took them and forced them past my tongue down into my throat. I heard a pop as soon as it got far enough. I moved the scissors around and around and heard endless pops. I think I was hitting air bubbles. The pain stayed strong.

The door creaked open and the doctor stepped in with a bottle of medicine and a spoon. He set it down and ran to me and grabbed the scissors out of my throat. He pushed me back into the seat and once again overpowered me and strapped me down. I was so dizzy from the flush of colors against my eyes I almost didn't put up a struggle.

He grabbed the medicine and poured it into the spoon, then stuck it in my throat. The liquid slowly drooped down my throat and it was as hot as lava. I tried to cough it up but it was impossible. I needed it out of my throat and all I could do was cough.

My worriedness caused more expanding in my throat, like I had a soccer ball trapped there. The air I attempted to breathe in struggled to get past the lump in my throat. My lungs were only filling up enough to just keep me going.

I couldn't think straight, I couldn't see straight, I was just there, mindlessly feeling the pain. How was I still clinging to life? I just wanted to clear my throat. I wanted to breathe. The doctor was just sitting there watching me, but my vision was too blurry to tell what else he was doing.

"Doctor... am... I... ok-ay?" I said between long breaths.

He replied, "There was never anything wrong with you."

"Doc-tor... you... can't... tell..." I paused to catch my breath, "me... noth-ing... is... wrong... l-look... at me..."

But he didn't reply to that. He grabbed the medicine again and fed me more. The pain in my throat got bigger and clogged up my throat walls. Tiny wheezes of air could still get through, but it was the smallest amount imaginable. The burning medicine seemed to be clogging up over the painful lump in my throat. The burning sensation stayed there, and I was sure my throat was going to melt clean through and my head was going to roll to the ground.

Then I passed out.

***

I was in a chair in the hallway when I woke up; just as empty as the first time I was in it. The pain in my throat was still there and so big I couldn't get any air to pass through. I fell from my seat and gasped for breath. I dug my short fingernails through the soft flesh around my throat. My fingers sank deeper and felt around the structures below the skin; warm blood caressed my shaking hands.

"The doctor will see you now." The silvery voice of a nurse calls from down the hall.

STORY FIFTEEN:

WONDERLAND

It was nothing short of magical for the two little girls when the special door appeared for the first time, and it wasn't any less beautiful when it appeared every day for the rest of the month. It took them up from the bedroom they shared into another room with a queen-sized bed and big windows on every wall. Each window had two metal bars across it except for the window above the bed. The room felt more like home than their normal room did.

They wanted to close the door behind them and never leave the view they had of the lovely meadow. The carpet of blue forget-me-nots had a hold on their imaginations, and they envisioned an ocean of pixies hiding between the flowers. Careful rays of sunshine meandered through the trees that were so tall they reached past the clouds, then fell into the stream of water like a cascading waterfall and illuminated the whirling and revolving tints and shades of color in the stream; pools of wine fell into pretty shades of plum, waves of green overtook rifts of pink, marigold faded to cider, and silver turned into taffy. A shadow from a tree fell perfectly along the freshly carved path to the wooden swing set that had never been there before.

The girls agreed to climb through the window for the first time. They got outside of the magical room without a single scratch on their unblemished skin. They saw the small building the room belonged to; it looked like any other house would, but that didn't take away from its mystifying aura.

A precious breeze hit them. One raced the other down the path that smelled like autumn to the swing set waiting for them. Neither girl had ever felt anything more enjoyable than the feel of the flowers under their feet. They sat down and swung.

The path was gone—it vanished in the tick of a watch. One girl turned to the other. Both cried. They jumped off the swings and pushed past the forget-me-nots that had taken the place of the path. The flowers grew taller every time the girls blinked and obscured their vision of the house. They'd never find the path again. They were lost in a wonderland of beauty forever.

STORY SIXTEEN:

THINGS NOT SEEN

The sweet nighttime darkness dwindled down the April skyline. The birds were silenced. Nothing walked the streets except for a thin mist. Evelyn Cochran lay in her bed, staring out the window at the empty blanket of sky. Occasional, cool breezes swept into Evelyn's room—her bed was right under the window—but she didn't mind.

A feeling too cold to be the wind rolled along her spine. Evelyn lay there petrified. A presence stood at the edge of bed and tugged on her, but she dared not to look. The freezing touch of fear tingled on her feet and played along her hands.

The presence shifted over Evelyn. Its icy arms traced Evelyn's body—she was encased in the cloud of unknown that hovered over her. Her eyes met the presence's eyes of indigo. Evelyn stared into them against her will; she was frozen.

The presence levitated her, inches above her mattress. Footsteps came down the hall. They pounded closer by the second. Her heavy heartbeats could've been footsteps themselves. Her eyes couldn't move to see who was coming.

The presence cradled Evelyn's small throat with both hands and pulled her against its sickly-cold body. A third hand slithered down Evelyn's face to her neck, and then down her arm, then studied her hand. It folded back her fingers all at once except for the pointer finger.

"Evelyn, Evelyn, Evelyn," a throaty voice whispered, "feel what I have felt."

The presence lifted Evelyn's outstretched finger and placed it inside the soggy bullet-hole wound that appeared inside her forehead. Timeless pain cracked inside of her.

Then the presence was gone.

STORY SEVENTEEN:

TROUBLE SLEEPING

So much for a good night's sleep.

I clicked the home button on my phone and nearly blinded myself as I tried to read the time. 2:39 AM. I tried to shut my eyes again but sleep wouldn't come. I heard a noise from outside my room. I paid it no mind and shifted in bed.

Nine sheep, ten sheep, eleven sheep, twelve sheep, thirteen sheep, fourteen—

Tink. Squeak. Thud.

The sound of a creaking floor panel and the thudding of steps upstairs.

Seventeen sheep, eighteen sheep, nineteen sheep, twenty sheep, twenty-one sheep, twenty—

Tink, squeak, thud.

A little more audible this time. Almost deliberate; as if somebody wanted me to know he was here.

Tink. Squeak. Thud.

Is someone toying with me? Are mom and dad up? They wouldn't be up so late and walking around making noise.

I sat up in bed and felt adrenalin set in at the thought of a stranger being in the house. It had to be a stranger.

Tink, squeak, thud.

Now the noise seemed to come from the next floor right above my room. I ran over to my closet—making more noise than I should've—and grabbed my baseball bat from against the all. I gripped it so hard I could already see the imprint of the wooden handle on my sweaty palms.

I tiptoed out of my room and to the hallway. Hidden, I waited beneath the stairs that led to the next floor. Surely no intruder would make it past me… but I heard no more noises and was curious, so after a few moments I climbed the stairs, careful to be as sly as possible, ready to swing my bat at the slightest movement.

I peeked into my parents' room. Both asleep. Maybe one of them had gotten up for something— after all, the bathroom light was still on… maybe one of them went to the bathroom and forgot to hit the switch.

I went back down to my room—my house as silent as it normally is—and put away my bat, then got into bed.

Where was I again? Twenty-…three? sheep, twenty-four sheep, twenty-five sheep, twenty-six sheep, twenty-seven shee—

Tink. Squeak. Thud.

Just as loud, just as deliberate, but closer than ever; still right above my room. I sneaked back out from under my covers and gently made my way to the light switch. I turned it on then grabbed my baseball bat and headed back upstairs.

I had to admit, I was a bit paranoid now. Either my parents were pranking me, or someone was really in here, and I hated either option—

A bit jittery, too—I just swung at a shadow. Go figure.

There's nothing hiding up here. I swear it's just my mind playing tricks on me. This search is going nowhere. Sigh. Too much stress from school or something, that's probably why you were hearing things. Damn senior year.

I left the upstairs after taking one last look into my parents' room. Neither had moved one bit. I put the bat away in the closet, shut off my lights, and went below my covers. I drank some of the day-old water on my nightstand. Creeping around in the dark really makes a guy thirsty.

Might as well surf the web since I'm up.

Tink, squeak, thud.

Not even my headphones would block out the noise…

Tink, squeak, thud.

And then I could see it: a malformed and misshapen head on top of a twisted neck looking down at me, its body bent in a way that should not be possible. Although the sockets were empty, I knew whatever it used as eyes were fixed on me.

Tink, squeak, thud… shatter.

Its foot kicked out the lightbulbs that hung from the fan.

Tink. Squeak. Thud.

It could walk on ceilings.

STORY EIGHTEEN:

MAGIC MIRROR ON THE WALL

Nighttime climbed down the sparkling heavens like a spider against a wall. Janel sat on a bench in front of a wishing well, her eyes transfixed on the stars and her mind dreaming of a better place in a better world.

Her hand reaches into her purse, and her eyes never waver from looking at the gorgeous dots of light in the sky. Once her hand finds the coin she was searching for, she makes her way to the rim of the wishing well, shuts her eyes, and plays with the silver in her hand until she makes a wish.

The coin sinks to the graveyard of change.

She opens her eyes and sees it there, heads-side up and looking back at her. She turns away and leaves for home.

***

She locks the door behind herself, then checks it twice to be safe—something she has done since childhood. Her home is unusually hot, but she doesn't mind—it is a beautiful contrast to the November air that had soaked her body.

Her bedroom is even hotter; she forgot to unplug the heater. She does so, then collapses on her bed.

So tired...

She undresses, then opens her wardrobe that brimmed to the ceiling, and finds pajamas. She walks back to her bed—the air at her feet beginning to drop from hot to warm—and sinks on top of her blue covers. She slides her head under the pillow, and as she drifts to sleep, the sparkles of her wish at the well flow into her room and cover her.

***

Her curtains mute any morning sunshine. She wakes up tired yet refreshed; the fancy mirror on the dresser against the wall opposite her bed makes sure she knows how messy her hair looks. She stands up and takes a step, then she realizes something...

Did I shut the door behind myself?

She twists the knob, but the door itself won't open.

Huh?

Again, she twists the knob, then pulls. There is no opening the door.

What is going on?

She twists and pulls with both hands, then puts all her body into pulling the door open, but it doesn't move a single hair-length. She is stuck inside her room.

"Why won't you open?" she begged, tugging on the knob. Panic shot through her temples and suddenly she has a headache. The butterflies won't leave her stomach alone.

"Janel?" a voice inside her room said.

She quickly turned towards the voice her heart beating like a jackhammer. Her stomach turns and her legs almost give out.

"Janel?" it says again.

Janel takes a step back. "Who's in here?"

"Come closer and see," the voice says. "It's just your mirror. Come closer and see."

She doesn't dare move.

"*It's just your mirror, Janel.*" it shouts, "*Come closer and see.*"

Her knees stutter and her heart twitches and her eyes swell with tears of fear; she couldn't have felt worse. Her legs begin moving, but each step feels like standing on burning asphalt.

"My mir- my mirror?" Janel says. Her whole body trembles until she gets close enough to see into the mirror. Her dark eyes look back at themselves.

"Uh..." Janel starts, then pauses.

There is a moment of silence until her mirror speaks, "Janel, you're the most beautiful woman I've ever had the pleasure to reflect."

Her reflection fades away as the mirror speaks. Janel backs away.

"I never want to reflect anybody else."

"What are you?" Janel asks.

It replies, "Your mirror."

"What do you want?"

"You."

She almost trips running away from the mirror and back to the door. Once more, it twists but doesn't open. She hits the door with her fists and the heavy pain shoots down in needle-like tingles to her elbows, and from her elbows to her shoulders. Her mouth his dry, her body craves water. She falls down, exhausted, and stares at the ceiling.

A kaleidoscope of colors intertwine and crisscross against the black plane of existence that her eyelids hold when she rubs them. She slowly gets back to her feet, then runs to the windows by her bed and bangs on them with tired hands.

"Help! Help me! Can anybody hear me?"

She tries to open them between tired breaths but it's no use; even while they're unlocked, there's no opening the windows.

"Anybody? Can anybody hear me? Help! *Help!*"

"They won't open," the mirror says.

Janel turns, frightened. The mirror is empty. There is an aura of hatred around it.

"I can't let you go."

Janel turns back to the windows and hits them with as much force as her hands can handle. The glass just won't break; it's as if it's made out of diamonds.

"Oh God! Please! Anyone? *Please!*"

"There's no leaving me, Janel."

She tries the door again in desperation, but already knows there's no escape from the wicked voice in the mirror. She feels smaller and smaller inside, and her fears became commonality. She is frantic, and grabs the heater and bangs it against the glass, but it doesn't make a difference. The window is still in perfect shape.

There has to be a way out.

She has about lost her mind. All she can do is sit on her bed and cry. The tears sting her dry eyes.

"Don't cry."

"Why not? You've got me held like a prisoner."

"Crying will ruin your gorgeous eyes, Janel."

"Shut up, mirror!"

"I told you, you're the most beautiful woman I've ever had the privilege to reflect."

"I don't care what you think." Her immense cries turn to depressing sobs. "I want to go."

"I can't do that. I want you, Janel. I need you."

"Well, I don't need you."

"Your lips are smooth threads of wine, and oh, how your eyes look like stardust sprinkled across the oceans."

Janel is confused—she has to hold back a smile.

Huh?

"Who could be more beautiful than you?"

"Well... thank you."

"How do you feel about it, Janel?"

Janel lowered her eyebrows, "About?"

"About what I said to you? About how I feel about you?"

"Uh, it's very sweet... very sweet... but please, let me go."

"There's no leaving me, honey. I want you."

"Can I please leave the room for a moment?"

The mirror replied, frustrated, "*No! No, I cannot let anyone else have you.*"

His voice made a whole new ocean of tears flood from her eyes.

"Hey now, don't cry. I told you, crying will ruin those gorgeous eyes. Do you know how beautiful you are, Janel?"

"No—no, I don't."

"You have this radiance that makes you irresistible to me."

"Let me g—"

"You're the masterpiece of all creation. Of anything the gods could piece together with all their infinite power, abilities, and creativity: it'd be you."

"I don't believe in a God or gods... I'm starting to wonder if this is all just a dream."

"If this is all just *my* dream then you're the best thing I could've created. If I dreamed you into existence, there's no masterpiece I can dream to outshine you."

"And that's nice of you to say... but really, you're a mirror, I'm a person, and I just can't—I just can't be with you."

"It's okay, my love."

Janel sobbed.

"I've watched you for a while... watched you laugh your whole life. And when you laughed, I couldn't help but smile and laugh with you. To watch you like that really made me happy."

Janel wipes her tears, "Mirror, I hope you know I can't take all these compliments. I just can't."

"You don't appreciate them? I thought you would. I see all the beauty supplies you have on your dresser, I see—"

"I do love beauty and I try my best, but how can I take compliments from a mirror holding me hostage?"

"Janel…"

"What?"

"I don't know. I just feel so passionate about you. I see a special kind of beauty in you."

"I feel you just like what you see on the outside. But I suppose that's all you can see. A mirror just shows you the outside. You like what you see of me, but you'd never see—you'd never *like* what's on the inside."

"I've watched you for a long time, I already said this. I've seen how you act when nobody is around, I've seen how you act when people are around. I know who you are and I love you."

"And just how long have you been watching me?" Janel asks, all her worry having left for sparse moments, and now creeping back into her.

"Your inner beauty is another reason I li—I *love* you."

"I asked you a question, mirror," she says, furious. "How long have you been watching me? I'm so confused here."

"Your whole life, darling."

"Have… have you been watching anybody else?" It is getting harder not to scream.

"Not as long as I've been watching you."

"Why me?"

"I've grown terribly attached to you. I hate when you leave and your beauty escapes me. I realized I never wanted to go a minute with you, so that's why I'm keeping you here with me."

"Don't you think that's a bit creepy?"

110

"I'm sorry, darling."

Janel yawned and looked back to the window, hoping somehow it'd be open and that she could jump out of it and get away from this mess. But it was still closed.

Foolish to think it'd be open, and—wait... it's night out? Already? But we couldn't have talked more than an hour...

"Jesus," she says., "Have we really been talking this long?"

"Time flies when you're having fun, doesn't it?" the mirror says, sounding so sincere that it pisses Janel off.

"I wasn't having fun, mirror."

Mirror replies but Janel ignores his words; she hates the sound of his voice, and all his compliments sound the same to her. She crawls under her covers, yawning again and again until she shuts her eyes and the beautiful layer of thick sleep takes over.

"Goodnight," the mirror whispers.

Her wish is coming true.

***

Her dry throat begs her for water when she awakes at 3 AM.

"Can't sleep?" the mirror asks.

"AH!" she screams. "Holy hell, how did you know I was up?"

"I know a lot of things, Janel," the mirror says. "Get some rest and clear your mind. You won't sleep with all that worry floating around."

Her eyes shut and she rests in bed, but sleep never comes. It is a paranoid few hours until she sees the sun come up. The mirror had been quiet the rest of the night.

Does he sleep? Maybe... I mean, he hasn't talked to me in hours. What if I catch him off guard?

She pulls away her covers and calmly steps out of bed. The whole room is muted—there isn't even the sound of breathing. She is as soundless as can be. Her feet move silently across the floor, and the feel of the knob turning in her hand is like a miracle.

Full of hope, she pulls the doorknob. And when it won't open, the mirror speaks to her. "It wasn't a dream. There's no leaving me."

"I'm begging you—"

"*No!*"

Just the evil sound of his voice makes her feel gross inside. She feels violated by her damn mirror. She walks back towards her heater, grabs it, then looks toward the disgusting mirror. Nothing reflected in it. She turns back to the windows and throws the heater at it and prays for a miracle.

Please God if you're real just--just make it open. Let me leave. Crack the window open. I need to—

But of course it doesn't break. The heater hits her bed, then tumbles to the floor with a loud crash and a snap; the insides of the heater clanks around and some pieces fall out. The heater is broken, and the warmth in her room grows suddenly thin.

"I'm sorry I made you feel so angry at me," the mirror says.

Janel looked to it—fists clenched and angry eyes twitching—then says, "Maybe I'd be less angry if you let me leave! This is no way to treat someone you claim to love." She sat down on her bed, then added: "So now what? I just sit here frustrated for forever while you bother me?"

"I want to shower you in compliments forever, dear."

"What kind of life is this, mirror?"

"The life I want."

"And how about the life I want?"

"You'll come to like this life, Janel... just you and me and happiness."

"I've already told you you're not what I want." She wants to explode. "Don't you want someone who'll love you back?"

"All I want is you."

An idea came to her. She went to her dresser—which was overflowing with mountains of beauty products and makeup—and opened the drawer that kept most of the junk she barely ever used. Her hand digs around for the yellow screwdriver. She smiles and ignores the words from the mirror as she walks over to the door.

The two screws in the knob look back at her like two angry eyes. She puts the screwdriver into the head of the first one; the screwdriver twists and so does the screw. That's all it ever does. It twists in either direction she tries but it never comes out. She tries the next screw. Same result. They turn and turn, and they could turn for all eternity and a day, but they'll never come out. She is never leaving the room.

"I could've told you that," the mirror says. "Never gonna happen."

Janel throws the screwdriver at the ground, "And why not?"

"Janel, you are mine."

She sighs and picks up the screwdriver. As desperate as can be, she goes back to the window and looks at the outside world. She expects it to sound like a clang when the screwdriver hits the window, but it sounds like a million icepicks dragging across a whiteboard.

"Oh, Janel, I've been craving you so."

That's when she loses it and throws the screwdriver at the mirror. There is an odd silence as its corner breaks and sparkling pieces fall between a handful of lipsticks.

Hope blooms inside of her and she goes back to the door, knowing it will open...

"It'll take more than that, gorgeous."

She breathes loudly; the anger is practically dripping off of her. She is absolutely broken inside. Something snaps in her head. She hops onto her bed and holds the pillow to her head and screams and screams and screams—such vile, devilish screams shouldn't have been possible but they leave her throat.

"You're so pretty when you're mad."

She turned to the mirror, still clutching her pillow, then yelled, "Shut up!"

"I'm sorry... but gosh, you're always so pretty. So radiant and stunning."

"I don't want to fucking hear it."

"Did I already tell you that if the whole sky were paper, there'd not be enough room to write about you?"

"Stop it. Please just stop. I can't take hearing all these compliments, all these nice things... I just can't."

"Why? Why not? They're true, you deserve to be told them."

"I don't deserve them and it gets annoying when you repeatedly just tell me I'm so fucking pretty."

"Janel, Janel, Janel... my darling Janel. Please understand, you've stolen my heart away."

"I didn't steal anything." Janel put her hands on her face, "Look at me. I'm talking to my mirror. I'm talking to my mirror. I've lost my marbles."

"Come on, marbles can be found."

Janel gets to her knees, then looks up to the ceiling.

"What did I do to deserve this? Why me?"

"Janel, if I may—"

"I didn't ask you!" she snaps.

"But my beautiful darling, my love, I—"

"Why don't you just die, Mirror?"

"If I died for you, there'd be no better way to go."

"Then do it."

"Ah, you can't get rid of me so easily,. We've hardly had time together. It's only been a few hours."

"Huh—hours? It's been over a day!"

"What's it matter how long it's been? All that matters is we have each other. You and me. You and me here until the end. Me and your succulent face."

"Can you think about something other than my face?"

"How can I, darling? My darling, there's nothing I'd rather be thinking about, nobody I rather be looking at."

"What happened to the last woman you did this to?"

"Nobody's beauty has ever entranced me to this level before you."

"If you like me so much, tell me how you can keep the door closed? And the windows? How can you possibly do any of these things?"

"One day I'll tell you. I wish to be with you forever, unraveling all your secrets… and you'll unravel mine."

"I have no secret."

"We all do, Janel."

"Tell me one of yours then."

"I wish I had a body. A human body."

"That's shocking. Why—why is that?"

"So I can hold you and feel your heartbeat and unlock the mystery of your lips with my own."

"Oh, spare me the bull. I don't need to hear these lies."

"But I mean it. What do I gain from lying?"

"My love? I don't know. You just wanna tell me what you think I wanna hear. But this isn't anything that I want. I don't want to do this. I don't want you or any of this. I want to leave this room and never come back. I never want to hear your annoying voice. I want my life back."

"Oh, Janel. You'll get over it."

Her scream tears through the silence like a sharp shard of glass tearing through soft flesh. She stands on her bed and bangs her hands on the windows.

"*I just want to get out of here!*" Janel screams. "*I just want to get out of here!*"

She collapses from exhaustion. Her eyes shut against her will.

"Get me… get me out… of… here…"

Janel is asleep.

Her wish is coming true.

***

"So gorgeous when you sleep." He wakes her up. "When you're so at peace, without a single care in the world. Ah, your beauty just grows and grows. Nobody can compare, my love, my darling, my sweet little Janel. So lovely, so cute, so perfect in every single way. So dazzling, so—"

"Ugh."

"What's on your mind, lovely?"

"Ways to escape."

"Baby, don't talk like that. That's crazy talk," the mirror says. "Ah, you look so gorgeous right now."

Janel ignores him and stares at the ceiling, hoping he'll just... vanish.

"You're stunning," he says.

She ignores him.

"How did I get so lucky to look at you for forever?" his voice sounds furious. "I want nothing more than this, to admire you for eternity."

She almost smiles when she hears how mad he sounds.

"Janel, don't ignore me please." And when she doesn't reply, "Honey? Janel, talk to me! Come on. Janel?"

Janel finally replies, "Maybe if I ignore the voices they'll all go away."

"There's no going away," the mirror says. "There's nothing to go away to. There's me, there's you, there's us, that's all there is and that's all that matters."

She ignores him once more.

"Janel, talk to me. *Talk to me!*"

She covers her face with the pillow.

"Dammit, Janel."

"I want to go," Janel says with severe sadness in her voice. "Just let me go."

"You want to know something?" the mirror asks.

"What?"

"I've got a secret to tell you."

"Then tell me," Janel says.

"I'll tell you—for a kiss."

"You're crazy. You're insane. You're a damn mirror."

"Just kiss me, lay your lips on me for a second and I'll tell you an important secret."

"About?" she asks, the curiosity rising in her voice with every word.

The mirror replies, "About you. About your wish and that wishing well."

"How did you know about that?" she finally looks his way.

"Kiss me and find out, Janel."

"I don't trust you, mirror."

"I want your lips more than anything. My thoughts always slip away when I look at them. They're alluring."

I don't deserve these compliments you give. I told you that."

"You deserve them and more. You deserve better descriptions than my words can ever give."

"Stop it."

"Janel, we've gotten off topic. Give me a kiss. One kiss. It's all I want, just a taste... and I want that taste to linger forever."

Am I really gonna do this?

She stands up and reluctantly walks to that accursed mirror. She stares deep into it, wondering where her reflection went and why the mirror no longer reflects anything in sight. It isn't quite like looking into glass—the mirror is definitely reflecting something, but that something looks like nothing and Janel felt confused with fear sprinkling into her mind.

She kisses it and enjoys the smooth coldness on her lips. It is more than the little kiss the mirror asked for. It probably lasts half a minute and she almost forgets to take her lips off the glass until she hears a moan coming from it—then she pulls away immediately.

I'm so dumb. How can I like that? Shit, I've lost my mind. Shit, shit, shit.

"Well?" Janel says.

"That was amazing and a lot more than I asked for. That was… I'll cherish that forever, little darling."

"Tell me that stupid secret you promised me, Mirror."

She couldn't have felt more humiliated than she does now.

"Well…" the mirror says, "I think you may know this, but that wish you made… I'm it, honey."

A look of realization plays upon her face, and a splash of fear plays upon her voice, "My wish. I- I—"

"Your wish in that wishing well. You wanted to be more beautiful. Don't deny it, Janel. That was your wish. You got your wish. You're irresistible, but only to me. I'm the only who'll know of your beauty."

"That—that's not—that's not true at all!"

"Why lie?" he asks.

Janel sobs, "I'm not! I'm not—I'm not lying."

"Janel."

"Fine!" she yells. "I wished it! I wanted to be more beautiful. That was my wish... my damn wish."

"And it came true!" the mirror says joyfully "So be happy! I'm here with you and I appreciate your beauty. So be happy, be mine."

"This isn't what I wanted... you're not what I wanted..."

"You've got to accept it, sweetheart."

"I want my life back, can't you understand?"

"No, it's you who doesn't understand." The mirror sighs. "You asked, you got. Deal with it."

"How was I supposed to know my wish would end with me locked in here for eternity? I want out! I want a life! I don't want you!"

"Haha. You asked and you received," the mirror laughs.

"Please, just let me go, I take back my wish. I take it back, dammit. I take it all back, I just wanna go!"

"No."

Janel cries, "I just wanna go! I just wanna go! I just wanna go!"

"It's funny, we're both sitting here with the situation we want, but it isn't going how we wanted."

"Then fix it!" Janel says. "Give me what I want. Just give it to me, Mirror."

"It'll be what we both want. In the end, it'll be what we both want, Janel."

"In the end? In the end what? When I'm crazy enough to start believing you? When I go insane? And that's if I'm not insane already."

Janel leaves the mirror and goes to the window. She presses her face and hands to it and dreams of being out there beneath the sunshine and caressed by the warm air.

"I just want the outside world," Janel says. "Life. A life. My life. Not trapped in a cage."

"Calm down, honey."

"It's not fair! It's not fair!" Janel pulls on handfuls of her charcoal-colored hair. "I just wanted a little more beauty, and this is what it costs me? It costs me my whole life? Trapped here in a box with an annoying voice?"

"Janel, my love, stop it! Stop it! Stop it!"

"I just wanted to be beautiful! I tried and tried, and I wanted to be special, but here I am! I'm insane."

"Calm down!"

"I bet the door and windows are wide open! I'm just too insane to realize it! I'm trapped here in a box!"

"You're not crazy, love. You're my darling. I keep you with me because I enjoy your presence."

"That's the only explanation. I'm crazy. I'm a crazy bitch."

"Calm down, my love."

Janel walks to the dresser, then leans over it, her face only a few inches from the mirror. "Calm down?"

"Yes," the mirror replies.

"Because you love me?"

"Yes, dear."

"You love me because of my face, right? My beauty?"

"Well, yes…"

"Do I have fair, clear skin?"

"You do, honey, but why do you ask? It's without a blemish."

"Because I want to hear you scream and cry, Mirror."

"What?"

Janel laughs as she picks up the nail clippers off her dresser. She raises them to her cheek without hesitation and clips off a small piece of skin. Two drops of warm blood race each other down her face. She clips off more pieces; blood traces over blood. She clips and clips, then fixates on the mirror. "What, nothing to say?"

"I'm just shocked..." the mirror replies.

She clips at least fifteen gorgeous times, each one unique and on its own. Her eyes grimace in pain and the bags under them grow heavy.

Have I done it? Is he done with me?

"Janel... what have you done?"

Janel smiles. "Do you love me even now?"

"I do. Nothing can make me dislike you. The perfect red color of your lips now paints your face."

Enraged, she grips the edges of the mirror and shakes, but it is much too heavy and much too sturdy to move. She wants to kill him.

"Let me go!" Janel wailed, *"I'm not beautiful anymore! You have no reason to hold me here!"*

"But you're stunning."

Her trembling hands slowly dig into the cuts— fingernails tearing the skin apart to make room first, then whole fingers slip inside. Her fingers slither around the burning interior of her cheeks, and her eyes roll back in pleasure. The cuts are much bigger, much deeper, and she is absolutely positive the mirror will hate her now.

"This—this is beautiful? This is beauty to you?" she asks.

The mirror replies, "Yes. I like your inner beauty too. I like you for you."

"You make no sense!" Janel says. "You said you just liked me for my face. I mutilated it and here you still are, feeding me bullshit you think I want to hear."

"It's something you need to hear, dear."

"I'm tired of your compliments!"

She puts one of her cuts to the mirror. "What's beautiful about this?"

"Everything," the mirror says. "Everything from how passionate you are down to the gorgeous shades and tints of red that play upon your skin and hair."

Janel pulls on her hair, then says through grinding teeth, "There's. Nothing. Beautiful. About. Me."

"Janel, you're being irrational. Just breathe. Breathe in and out slowly."

Janel listens. She breathes in and out slowly.

"You're beautiful, Janel, no matter what you do to your face."

Janel cuts out more slivers of flesh. Oh, how she enjoys it. She can feel the mirror's heart being crushed with every snip.

"Janel…"

"What? What, Mirror? What?"

"I still love you."

Janel punches the mirror. Splinters of glass embed in her skin. It doesn't faze her. The remaining pieces of glass hanging from the frame seem to taunt her. She can already predict the annoying compliments the mirror is bound to say. She searches the top of her dresser for the biggest piece of glass there is, then closes her palm around it— light as a feather at first. She takes a deep breath. The glass stings to the touch, but she squeezes it; she lets go of any emotions and all feelings and just squeezes. Her palm turns as red as anger.

"Don't keep hurting yourself, my love. You're my life, Janel. Don't do this."

Janel presses the point of the glass on her forearm a couple inches away from her elbow, *"I am not your life!"*

She traces it down to nearly her wrist, then grimaces again. She not only feels pain, but regret. She looks back to what is left of the mirror and the mirror finally shows her reflection. She is too embarrassed to look at herself.

The glass turns to tiny pieces when she throws it at the wall.

"What am I doing?" she asks.

"Something foolish, my love. You're hurting your beautiful body."

Her legs shake, her breaths are heavy; she hangs onto the dresser like a person drifting at sea would hold onto a piece of driftwood.

"Are you okay?" he asks.

"I won't be okay until I'm out of this room," she says.

She collapses with the clipper in her hand. She shuts her eyes and her head spins on a rollercoaster through a thousand tiny loops. Slowly, she opens her eyes back to her room and sits up, staring at the nail clippers.

She stretches out the arm she had cut with the glass then cut out snippets of skin with the nail clipper; her cuts look like a flower with falling petals.

"I'll do whatever it takes until you set me free," she says. "None of this is beauty. It's all disgusting. I'm disgusting. I don't even wish to be beautiful anymore. Just. Set. Me. Free."

"Everything you just said is impossible," he replies.

"No it is not!" she screams.

She stabs her arm with the nail clipper like an animal acting on instinct. A flash of white passes before her eyes and her whole body feels unusually warm. She tears up more of her skin as she pulls the nail clipper out, then throws it at the godawful mirror.

"I am so tired of you. So damn tired."

"But my love—"

"I want you to die! Just die already!"

"I can't die," the mirror says. "Not when my purpose is to reflect your beauty forever. There's no other purpose for me, nothing greater than reflecting you and capturing your beauty for myself. Don't be mad. It's what you wanted."

"Oh, no, this is not what I wanted. No, no, no," she cries. "Mirror, please understand me! I just want you to understand me for a simple moment."

"But I've never misunderstood you, dear."

"That's all you've done, you idiot." She struggles to prop herself up, but when she does, she looks back to the mirror and says, "I hate you."

"I love you."

All it takes is four punches to totally destroy the remaining parts of the mirror. She breaks it, expecting something fancy to be hiding behind the glass, but there is nothing.

"I'm still here and you are still mine!" the devilish voice of the mirror screams.

"Why won't you die?" Janel sobs.

"Because you and I... because you and I are eternal."

"Stop it."

"How many times are we going to go around in circles, Janel? It's always the same thing with you. How long are you going to push me away? Be mine. Only mine. For eternity. I love you, Janel."

"Stop it, stop it."

"I can't stop. I have everything I could ever want right in front of me. You're mine and that's how things are going to be."

She grabs a handful of glass then throws it. She doesn't even know what she is trying to accomplish, but it makes her feel good. She lies down in the fetal position, blood staining her clothes, and pain and depression staining her soul.

"Die. Just die. Just die, Mirror."

"Why don't you want to be with me?"

"Because life is more than being locked in a box and hearing your endless compliments. I want to be free, people aren't meant to be kept in cages."

"Is it really a cage if you're with the one you love?"

"I never loved you and I never will."

"It isn't a cage to me. I love you."

"Shut up about love. Shut up about it all."

"But Janel—"

"But nothing."

Janel stands up and leans over the dresser to look at the broken pieces of glass. She bangs on them with her fists and throws handfuls at the wall.

"Just die!"

"Janel, don't do that!"

"Why don't you just die? Just die!"

She throws the biggest remaining piece of glass at the floor then smashes it with her bare feet.

"You're being irrational."

"Does it make you like me less?"

"Well…"

"Does it?"

"Oh, how could I stop loving you? It's impossible. All I want is you."

That is the last straw. She grabs her makeup and lipstick and nail polish and throws them all at the walls. She throws her hair straightener, too, and anything else she can find that is related to beauty. She is done with looks.

"Darling, what does that solve?"

"If I could smash you to smaller pieces, I would." She grabs what glass there still is and crushes it in her hands. "Die!"

"I'm still here, Janel."

"What will it take for you to die?"

"We're together forever, darling."

"Die! Just die, you fucking mirror!"

"Hahaha. Oh, Janel. Can't you see you're perfect to me? And can't you see that I can't die? You keep banking on the chance to either kill me or make yourself ugly, but it's obvious neither thing works. Yet you keep trying."

Janel stares at the mirror frame, "Am I really listening to some ghost of a mirror? I am insane."

"If you're insane it's because you keep doing and trying the same things over and over again, knowing full well the outcome will be no different."

"Stop trying to be some wise guy."

"Hey, you're the one trying to reason with a mirror."

She punches the frame of the mirror. *"I want out of here! Dammit let me out!"*

The mirror laughs. "Oh, Janel, Janel, Janel…"

"I just want you to die."

"And I want you to love me like I love you, sweetheart."

Janel opens her dresser drawer and finds a nail file. Even though the mirror is shattered, he can somehow see it.

"What are you going to do with that?"

"I'm gonna ask you a question, okay Mirror?"

"Okay, shoot."

"You said you'd always love me." She puts the nail file on the bottom socket of her right eye. "But could you love a lady with only one eye?"

With no hesitation and before he can speak, she forces the file up through the socket and through the slimy eye muscles. It makes such a horrible noise that seems to somehow echo inside the messy room. It takes a little pulling, but she moves the file out hard enough to pull the eye from its socket. It dangles like a body from a noose as she slides the nail file out. She smiles, taking the eye in her left hand and holding the file with the right, then slowly cuts it off from the cord it dangles by.

"I said, 'could you love a lady with one eye?'"

"Yes, my love. Yes. I can because I love you, and I wish you'd love me."

"Why can't you give up? Leave me be! I don't love you!"

"I've given you as happy a life as possible. I've given you the endless beauty you've always dreamed of. You should thank me."

"You've ruined me! Just die!"

"What did I do? I sat here and told you, you are stunning and amazing and wonderful and perfect. But you didn't like that. And instead of accepting responsibility, you went and hurt yourself. Everything that you are now, everything that you've done—it's been entirely on you."

"I don't wanna hear this."

"Because it's true."

"Fuck you!"

"Insult me all you want, it doesn't bring back your eye."

"I fucking hate you! I hate you! I hate you! I want to die! I want to die! I want to die! I want to be free of you and this room!"

"I don't know what to say."

"Say you'll let me be, let me free."

"I can't do that, Janel."

"I'm begging you, I've begged you endlessly already, just let me be free!"

There is one last shard of glass left that isn't completely in bits. Janel picks it up and goes to the mirror frame, and looks at it as though she is looking deep into the eyes of another person. She sighs.

"Mirror... I think you know that there's only one way this can go."

"Janel, don't you dare."

"Why not? It's better than to be trapped with someone I don't want. I've gotten more pain from you than from the stuff I've done to myself."

"That can't be true."

"But it is. Just let me go and I'll live and you can watch me in secret, okay?"

"I don't want any other soul to see you. You're only for my eyes, Janel dear."

She holds the glass to her wrist. "Then why shouldn't I do this? It'll make me happy, make me free, and it'll put you in pain. It's what's best for me. Can you see that?"

"No," the mirror says.

"You've ruined me," Janel cries. "You've ruined what you love."

"I didn't do a thing."

"You've ruined me, and there's only one way to separate us, Mirror."

"There's no separating us. Together forever. You and me to eternity."

"There never was a you and me."

"You're too chicken to kill yourself, Janel. I've watched you a long, long while. I know you can't do it."

She traces the glass shard over her wrist just to taunt the mirror. "Trust me, I'll do it. I'll do it."

"You shouldn't. Your life will end, but I'll still be here. You don't win at all."

"I'll be free of you."

"And at what cost, darling?"

She digs into the faint scratch she made, just a little deeper, "I—"

"Don't do it! Don't you dare do it!"

"Or what, mirror? I'll be dead, there won't be a thing you can do. Not a thing you can torture or threaten me with."

"I know you want to live. You'd rather live. Your first thoughts were 'let me out', not 'let me die'."

"Sometimes we gotta go with plan B," Janel said.

"What?" the mirror shouts. "This is like you skipped plan B and went straight to Z!"

"You've never left your plan A. You've been obsessed with me and wouldn't budge. Why should I? Why should I give in?"

"Because you're mine and I don't want to lose you. Can't you see you're all I have?"

She cuts a little deeper.

"Stop it now!" the mirror says. "There's still time to—"

"To what?" Janel asks. "Make you leave? That's all I want.

"It pains me to see you so hurt, love."

"This pains you?"

"It does. It does, okay? I wish you wouldn't hurt yourself. I don't want you to die and I don't want you to be hurt."

Janel sets the glass down on the dresser and is disgusted with herself.

"Good, Janel. Now destroy it and never touch another piece of glass. I'll take care of the mess some way, somehow."

Janel stares into the empty mirror frame.

"Janel?"

"Yes?"

"Did you hear me?"

"Sorry, Mirror, I was lost in thought."

"Break it. Break that last piece of glass and never cut yourself with it again, okay? Can you do that for me?"

Janel doesn't listen. She takes her shirt off instead.

"Whoa."

"You like that?" she asks.

"I love that," the mirror replies.

"I bet you do."

"I love you."

Quickly, she grabs the piece of glass and cuts across her chest. An explosion of pain runs through her skin and crawls into her bones.

"Shit," the mirror says.

"Am I still beautiful to you? Is this still beautiful?"

"Ye-yes."

She pushes the glass into the cut on her chest, then turns it clockwise. The pain doesn't matter; she is happy. She almost falls over laughing. She expects the mirror to say something, but he doesn't. Then, she puts the glass to her belly and cuts a couple straight lines that look like an equals sign—it is rough and the skin tears up in random spots, but she gets the job done. The final mark she makes is a curved one right below the vertical slashes, turning them into a smiley face.

"My darling, please, I'm begging you to stop doing this! You don't have to torture yourself!"

"What did you do when I begged? I begged and pleaded but you didn't budge. I'm not torturing myself, I'm torturing you."

She sits down on her bed takes her pants off and looks down at her thighs.

"Got a good view?" she laughs.

She stabs herself; a fountain of russet blood squirts out and dapples the floor. She cuts up and down with such elegance, as if she has a brush in her hand and is painting a canvas into a beautiful sunset. She laughs and smiles.

"*Enough! Enough!*" the mirror shouts.

"Mirror, baby, I'm just getting started," she laughs.

The glass is two inches into her thigh before it snaps in half.

"Oops!" she says, then slams her fist on it to send it down even further. It is a wishing well of blood escaping her body.

"This is insane," the mirror says.

Janel replies, "Baby, maybe I am insane."

Somehow she can still use her legs. She stepped through the puddle of blood and walked up to the empty mirror frame, "You can see clearly even when in a million pieces, right?"

"Yes."

She leans in, an inch from the frame. "Tell me what you see."

"What?"

"I said, 'tell me what you see.'"

"Well... I see the love of my life."

"Describe her to me."

"You have an ocean of raven-black hair I want to drown in."

"And I ripped some of it out, didn't I?"

"You have fair skin... as radiant and warm as the sun."

"And I tore out pieces of it with the nail clipper."

"The most gorgeous eyes of indigo."

"And I plucked one right out."

"That's it."

"Come on baby, that's the best you got?" she winks.

"I see the lips I've been blessed to feel."

"Lips, huh?"

"Yes."

"How much do you like 'em, Mirror?"

"Please don't do anything irrational, please don't do anything to them, please don't—"

"How much do you like 'em?"

"They mean the world to me, okay? You mean the world to me."

"I just wanna make 'em perfect for you. I just wanna apply a little color."

"As long as that's all you're doing..."

Janel purses her lips as if to apply lipstick, but holds the shard of glass to them, instead.

"Oh Lord, don't do it, Janel!"

"I have a question, Mirror."

"Yes?"

"Magic Mirror on the wall, who's the fairest of them all?"

"You—you are!"

"Are you sure about that?"

"I am. I am sure, now stop toying with me."

She traces her lips ever so slightly with the glass, being sure not to cut them just yet.

"Janel stop!"

Her light tracing becomes a furious slashing. The glass tears through her beautiful threads of red.

"Janel!"

Even though her lips are gone, she still traces. It is as though she is applying endless layers of lipstick. Blood gushes and falls to fragments of the mirror that lay below her.

"Am I not beautiful, darling?"

"Oh, what've you done? What've you done, Janel?"

"I'm as beautiful as I've ever wanted to be."

"You're hideous now! I'm sorry, love, but you're ugly!"

"Aw, mirror, you really think so?" she sets down the glass. "So can I go, then? Will you set me free? Let me get out of this room?"

"Janel… Janel, Janel, Janel."

"What?"

"I can't do that. I still want you to be mine and only mine. I made you a promise and I'm keeping it. You only stay with me. Always. Mine and nobody else's, nobody else gets to lay an eye on you."

Janel cries, "But why? It isn't fair! it isn't fair!"

"It's fair to me. I told you what was happening. You're mine, there's never going to be an escape."

"I hate you."

And with that, Janel slices her throat. Her ghost is gone from her body by the time she hits the ground.

***

Sunshine swept over her body the next morning. Her heater was running on full blast; her face was catching most of it. The door to her room was wide open, and as she lay there dead. The mirror was never broken.

STORY NINETEEN:

THE HOUSE OF BLUE LIGHT

It was obvious that a lot of time, money, and love had been invested into the lavish house and garden on 713 Wichmann Drive. The faint brushstrokes of fresh paint upon the window sills arched across the curved beams with a surreal precision, while the contrast between the muted tones of the home itself and the flowers artfully placed about its foundation offered a welcoming sense of natural disorder. Crushed limestone was spread out across the side yard, leading to a delicately laid out path, twisting between invisible barriers to the immense hedged garden in the rear of the home. It was here where the family cat, McKenzie—who was all black, save for the white back left leg—lived and could be found lounging in the sparkling beams of sunlight that broke through the canopy of oaks that lined the far side of the property.

Inside the bedroom that overlooked this beautiful garden on this beautiful night was April Mayberry. The rim of the well of darkness lived below her bed, its only inhabitant—The Shape. When the air feels too inconsistent—too hot yet too cold—he's there.

On September 7th, April Mayberry heard the whispers. Instead of counting sheep, she counted the narrow wooden boards that made up her bedroom's ceiling—as many as she could before the boards escaped the meager moonlight that slipped into her room and stayed in the unsure darkness. When she counted the last ones—as sleep was drifting upon her—something spoke to her and she told the whispers of her problems, and they listened. She grew attached to the whispers... all she had to do was give up a bit of her mind.

She cradled herself beneath toasty covers. The moon was still shining—very faint, but still shining. Her eyes drifted back to the woodgrains in the ceiling panels, and she started to yawn but suddenly became still—there was a woman crawling and clawing inside the wood. She was sure of it.

She didn't sleep. She was terrified of the woman she had come to watch for hours, who was crawling across her ceiling inside of the wood—and as she watched, a warmth inside of her grew. It was just a pebble at first, but by the time she sat up in bed, it consumed her. She needed to touch the lady in the wood. She needed to see if she were real.

She tried to reach the woman in the sea of hardwood, but every time April was about to touch the boards, the woman would move away. Frustration grew and April got angry. She ran around her whole room, blinded by darkness and hoping the woman would slip up so April could touch her. There was an indescribable maze of claw marks engraved into her bedroom walls. It had to be real.

The woman inched down to the foot of the closet door. April knelt down and touched her—scalding her fingers. The woman walked around the edges of the room—still inside the wood—and April followed until she lost sight of her.

Where did she go?

April went back to her bed. She cleared her mind of any thought of the woman and listened to the whispers. The calming, beautiful whispers.

She spoke, and the whisper's reply was faint.

Huh?

She called again to the whispers. The whispers said goodbye.

Don't leave me.

A new feeling of unreality fell over her. The whispers—her only friend—would never return. And in that new feeling of unreality, her mind blurred, and she felt like that lady in the wood panels. She raised her hands—seeing them through her own eyes as claws—and put them to her face; her nails clawed into her flesh that tore as easily as putty. Her fingers snapped through strands of muscles, and the chestnut red that blanketed her glistened in the last remains of dazzling moonlight. April herself then traced along the walls, acting just like the lady she had seen.

***

The Shape found Jonah McCoy hidden in a mostly void hallway behind a badly painted table—his breaths heavy, his tired mind racing. Hot and cold air wrapped around him. Unbeknownst to him, it's none other than The Shape.

He knew his minutes were numbered. He tipped over the table—as if that would do anything—and made a run for it to the nearest room—the bathroom. He was under the false impression that he was safe in here, thinking he'd just sleep in the tub then wake up in the morning and laugh... but as soon as his body relaxed in the tub... he knew The Shape had found him.

There wasn't even a chance to scream, because The Shape moved out from below the tub and grabbed him.

***

Billy Nelson had his left shoulder pressed against the front door of his house. He knew someone was breaking in, but he couldn't see them or hear them. The door was locked; no one was opening it from the outside—no one was even *standing* outside—but he knew someone was breaking in.

He strained as his muscles tensed and tired. His shivering feet slid out from under him and his right elbow landed beneath all his weight. He was in pain. What made it worse was the damned floor felt burning to the touch, as if a fire was contained inside of the floorboards and reached up in invisible cords that tangled over his body and held him to the ground. The air felt freezing all around him. His eyes darted from the lock, up to the obscured glass, and back. The Shape found him.

***

The first house on New Garden Boulevard waited for Stephanie Wernock—the gorgeous seventeen-year-old lady who was returning home from her typical Thursday-evening therapy session. She silently entered the home—being careful to avoid her family—then went to her bedroom.

For an hour, she sat in complete silence. She had schizophrenia—amongst other things—and had ignored her medicine for weeks. Stephanie was insane, and today the world was gonna see just how insane she was.

She locked her window, then went into her sleeping sister's room and locked hers, too, then the bathroom window, then the one at the end of the hall. She crept around the house as silent and as could be and locked every door or exit there was.

And when she was done, she stood still in the kitchen, staring at the array of sharp knives that were on the counter. Her hand slowly reached for one, then gripped it so hard her fingers turned pale. It was time she used it on them all.

She walked out of the kitchen when the cold air twirled around her and crisscrossed with strands of warm air. The feeling of The Shape washed upon her. She dropped the knife where she stood, then ran up the carpeted steps and into her room. She opened the window as fast as possible and jumped to her death.

***

Twins shifted in their cradle like a gentle wave that hits the shore. Two babies, so innocent and precious. But The Shape doesn't care for the innocence of a little baby. The Shape reached for the twins, and their whole existence slipped away.

***

Even as you've turned the page to this very point, you've felt The Shape drifting close and close to your fingertips. His whispers were stained throughout every story, and if you're lucky enough, he just might get you.

STORY TWENTY:

WHERE DID SHE GO?

Sixteen-year-old Alice Nolan walked inside her house feeling uneasy and disturbed. Every time she went outside, it seemed her neighbor Jerry Sinclair would go outside too—as if he were watching and waiting for her to go outside.

He can never get it through his fucking head.

She hated recalling any interaction with him but it was on her mind and wouldn't stop bothering her. He was insane—the look of anger he gave her was one that she could never forget; his eyes were glued to her, he didn't even blink. His lips made a straight line and his cheeks turned cherry red. Frustration was written on his popping veins.

"Oh, just leave me alone," she had told him. "Please, Jerry."

And in the most disgusting voice, he had told her, "I'll keep my distance, but I always got my eyes on you."

Alice shivered.

***

A week later, her parents were gone for the night. She took a shower after her lonesome dinner of takeout; the water as hot as hellfire. Her blue robe was fuzzy and oddly cold, a beautiful contrast to the hot water she had showered in.

She lay down on the couch with a blanket and put on a comedy. It was hardly 10:00 PM, but she was exhausted. Yawns wouldn't stop as she shut her eyes—

What was that?

A soft swoosh that sounded like someone stepping on carpet made her eyes open. She was petrified as she clenched the blanket close to her chest; only her eyes moved.

It was nothing.

She finally got off the couch—pretending not to be scared—and walked around the living room, then the kitchen.

See? Nothing.

She poured a glass of water; her mouth and lips were dry and it was so refreshing. She filled it back to the top, then took it back with her to the living room. There was someone hiding next to the couch.

Her hands trembled. The blood rushing through her hands felt like a thousand needles. The person's shadow started to move. She took a step back and found it hard to breathe—her lungs wouldn't move.

She dropped the glass and it shattered in every direction. She shrieked when Jerry—sunset red and angry—rushed towards her out of the shadow, his dark eyes locked onto her.

Alice ran out the front door. Jerry had to dodge the glass, so that slowed him down. Alice rang the doorbell of Jerry's house to tell his parents what he had done, and amid her fourth frantic ring, he grabbed her by the mouth and the waist.

Alice blacked out, but when she came to, she was tied to Jerry's bed with a rope. Jerry pulled out his sharp, gleaming pocketknife. The button he pushed made the spring push the blade upward. Jerry had his way with Alice.

"Keep screaming," he said. "That makes it even better."

He began to slice her up as he progressed. He lowered himself to Alice's lips. He kissed all the way down her neck and her chest, and up to her cheeks. After each kiss, he made incisions.

And as he held the knife to her throat—life already leaking from her body—The Shape came for them both.

STORY TWENTY-ONE:

STONE ROAD

There's never anything to do in Baylake, Kansas—the kids are practically *always* bored. The wide and dusty streets ran between blocks and blocks of rundown buildings as dry gusts of winds walked along them more than people did. The most interesting thing to do around there is to sit by the out-of-use train tracks and watch the mucky grass die.

***

Something was different about the darkness tonight—it wasn't the overflowing clouds blocking the moon, or the sickly cold that trailed the wind—it was just the mere sight of it. Night had come early today.

Even the air felt disgusting today—at least that's how it felt to Lucas Dyer as he sat in the passenger seat of his cousin Frank's car. Lucas was nervous as he read the sign that said *Lavenworth Road*. Lavenworth Road was nicknamed Stone Road, because that's where all the kids went to get stoned, though Lucas had never smoked a day in his life.

Their twenty-five minute drive came to an end when they parked in the driveway of a new-looking home. A brick path led to the colossal building. The leafless branches on the trees placed on either side of the home danced against the thinnest moonlight, looking like monstrous, skeletal claws scraping against a sky they could never reach. The rusty hinges of the mailbox creaked annoyingly.

Then, after just a moment, another car pulled up next to theirs. It was Frank's friends, Micah and Jake—people Lucas had met before but weren't really his friends—with three girls Lucas had never seen before. Jake was lean, tall, and handsome. Micah was the Jake wannabe—almost a jock, almost handsome, almost funny. Micah tried way too hard. He was almost like Lucas, a geek who didn't know how to change from geek to cool.

After greeting each other, they went inside the house. Lucas was on the tail end of the group and didn't see who had the key to this place. It was void on the inside, with bright white walls devoid of any trim. The glossy floors were made of that fake wood stuff. To the left was an unfinished kitchen, and to the right was a lengthy hallway that led down to the room where everyone was headed.

The room was almost as unfinished as the other parts of the house, except for the blue couches. The seven of them all found spots to sit down, but Lucas somehow found himself sitting alone and then feeling awkward when someone started rolling a blunt. The girl closest to him offered him a hit after she took one, but he declined.

"Did you bring your Ouija board?" That same girl asked another girl, holding back a laugh and a smile.

"Look, if you wanna conjure up some demon spawn from the great beyond, that's cool with me, just wait for me to leave before you start," Lucas said.

"Oh, we're just kidding," she told him. She could tell how uptight he was by his heavy sigh of relief. "Or am I?"

"Funny," Lucas said. "I'm Lucas."

"I'm Janel." she said. "This is my sister Lauren, and this is Paige."

Janel Payton's hair was russet and down to her back. From under the bangs that swept her forehead peeked lively hazel eyes that studied him. Lauren looked slightly similar, but her hair was shorter and less russet. She was taller than Janel but not anywhere near as gorgeous. The black eye shadow around her eyelids gave her a mysterious look. Paige's eyes were green and dazzling, and something about them set her apart from the other girls. Her lips were smooth threads of red wine. Her long brown hair stopped right below her shoulders.

"So what do you do?" Lucas blurted out, trying to sound confident but totally unsure what to say.

"What do I do?" Janel asked, confused.

"Well, uh, I mean—"

"I like comedies," she said. "Do you know the guys from school, or?"

"Frank's my cousin," said Lucas.

Lauren passed the blunt to Janel. Janel took a hit, coughed, then offered it to Lucas.

"I, uh… sure." Lucas grabbed it. "I, um, never smoked before. Ever. So I'm not sure what to do…"

Paige chuckled, "Just hold it between your lips and take a hit."

"And hold in the smoke for as long as you can. You'll get a better high that way," Frank added in. "Don't be scared to cough a lot, because the more you cough the higher you get."

Lucas held it between his fingers.

"Um…"

"Oh my God," Frank said, "just put the end of the blunt in your mouth and try to smoke it."

It made no sense to Lucas, but he tried it. It burned his throat and he tried not to spit everywhere. Lucas turned red as everyone laughed. He took another puff and held in the smoke.

This is torture, how does anyone like this?

He let the smoke escape his lips. He felt no different.

Lucas handed it to Micah. "I really don't feel anything, to be honest."

"How?" Frank said, "Maybe you just didn't do it the right way, but it's the best feeling in the world! You'll be so relaxed and everything'll be funny."

"It's not all it's cracked up to be," Janel said.

"So," Jake took a hit, "if a blind person has a dream, can they see it?"

"Why wouldn't they?" Paige replied.

"You're an airhead." Lucas laughed.

"What?" Paige said.

Shit.

"Sorry, I mean, uh, they can't see… so why would they be able t'see a dream," Lucas explained.

"Oh."

"Jake, pass the blunt," Frank said. "You always hog it."

Paige got up and sat down next to Lucas. He felt so nervous that he had to put his hands in his pockets so nobody could see them shaking.

"Hi, Lucas."

"I like your shirt, Paige." He smiled.

She looked down, as though to remember what it was. "Oh, you're a Cage the Elephant fan, too? I love them. I've very passionate about music."

"Me—me too."

"I actually just started learning guitar. Music is my biggest passion... y'know, besides stuffing a whole pizza down my throat."

Lucas laughed. "What—what, uh, types of music do you like?"

"I listen to all music, I'm not picky about genres," Paige said. "Anything from Elvis to NWA."

"Same here," Lucas said. "I love music from all different years and genres. I'm not much into country, though. That's probably the one I can't get into... do you like Motown?"

"Yes!" she said rather excitedly. "I love Motown. I like the feel to old music."

"Do you prefer AC/DC or Metallica?" Lucas asked.

Paige replied, "I love Metallica. I saw them in concert once. AC/DC is okay."

"What's your favorite Metallica song? Mine's Devil's Dance."

"Don't laugh at me," she said, "I know it's overplayed but I have to pick Enter Sandman."

"I'm jealous you got to see them in concert. I've never been to a concert... or like, anywhere else. I got invited to a concert once, but my friends bailed on me. This was back when I lived in New Castle. I'm actually from Pennsylvania... but New Castle was a bad city, so my parents decided to move to boring ol' Baylake, Kansas."

"You miss it?" she asked.

"Yeah. You from Baylake?"

"Nope. We moved here from Lubbock when I was... three?" she said. "I don't really remember it."

"You ever traveled anywhere else?" Lucas asked.

Paige replied, sort of laughing, "Just the area between here and Lubbock, mostly. What about you?"

Lucas wasn't sure if she always laughed this much or if it was from the weed. Probably the latter. "Same as you. Just been to New Castle and here."

"Really?" she said. "Not even New York? That's right above Pennsylvania."

"Nope," Lucas said. "And you've really never gone anywhere else?"

"Well," she said, "I mean, I've been to Oklahoma, Arkansas, Colorado, and Missouri... but they're nothing special. I think this section of the States is the boring section that's smashed between the states people actually care about."

"Probably right," Lucas said.

Lucas didn't know what to say as the conversation turned to a bit of an awkward silence. It was then that he noticed Frank was knocked out and snoring on the farthest couch, and everyone else had left the room. But just then, Jake and Janel entered the room again.

"Well, it's time to go now, Paige," Janel said, then called to Lauren to hurry up.

Lucas walked over to Frank then shook him. "Wake up."

Frank stared at Lucas, then uttered a few noises that Lucas couldn't understand.

"Wake up," Lucas repeated, feeling embarrassed for some reason. He was always embarrassed and nervous.

"What?" Frank said.

"You passed out. We're all going now."

"Damn."

Lucas turned to Paige, who was leaving alongside her friends. "Hey, Paige, it was nice to meet you," he smiled.

"It was fun," Paige replied.

Everyone left the house. Lucas was on the tail end of the group again. He noticed how nobody locked the door. Anybody at any time could just walk right into this place. He watched as Jake, Janel, Micah, Lauren, and Paige all left in Jake's car. He wished he could've talked to Paige a little bit more. There was something about her—she was just so nice. He wasn't used to having a stranger be so nice to him.

I should've asked for her number.

He sat down in the passenger seat and looked out the window to the night sky. The nighttime air still felt so different—the darkness in the sky looked wicked. Something unusual was floating above Baylake.

"So what did you think of your first time getting high?" Frank smirked.

"Meh, it seemed okay I guess. I didn't really feel anything," Lucas said.

"You probably just didn't do it right." Frank yawned, "So what did you think of the girls?"

"Janel and Paige are cool, I didn't really talk to Lauren. She was kinda quiet," Lucas said, tired.

"So you and Paige, huh?" Frank said.

"I wish," Lucas said.

"You don't think you have a chance?" Frank asked.

"I'm not sure. I think she was just being nice to me. Hard to tell if she was actually interested."

"I'll see when the guys are trying to hang next, and I'll invite her."

"You don't really have to do that."

"Listen, Lucas, we both know you're struggling in the lady department."

"You think I struggle, Frank? You fell asleep."

"Don't make me drop you off right here and have you walk the rest of the way," Frank teased.

They didn't talk for the rest of the ride back to Lucas's house.

Frank pulled up to Everette Avenue.

"Sorry about what I said, by the way," Lucas said as he left the car. "Wasn't trying to be rude."

"It's okay. I'll call you if we make more plans."

Lucas walked up the cement path and steps. The chipped railings and doors desperately needed to be repainted. The fading color of the bricks was depressing. The house was only a dump on the outside, though—the inside was beautiful and neat and practically always clean. His nose caught the scent of whatever his mom had cooked—he didn't care what it was, he just needed to eat; he was endlessly hungry, but it wasn't from the munchies.

After eating, he went upstairs and into his room. It was as vibrant as a gray-colored paint job could be. This was probably the only messy part of the house; his two dressers had more stuff on top of them than in them. He didn't change his clothes or shower; he jumped on his bed with his shoes still on and played back the day's events in his head like he always did, going over what happened and what he could've done differently. He was asleep after ten minutes.

***

He woke the next day a few minutes past noon, but his brain was still mushy. He had to lie there for a while before the fog of sleepiness went away. He grabbed his phone from the nightstand and caught up on notifications.

Gosh, do I smell bad.

Lucas gathered his clothes for a shower. There were two showers in his house, the nicer one on the main floor, and the average one on this floor. It was a lazy morning, so he picked this one. The water was just south of scalding.

He crawled back into bed after he finished. He shut his eyes and drifted in and out of sleep for an hour until the sound of his phone went off.

It was Frank.

"Hello?"

"We're all going back to Stone Road tonight. You down?"

"I—I guess so. I don't care about smoking… to be honest, I'm just going so I can see Paige."

***

Lucas looked at the time after hanging up. 1 PM. He had no plans besides whenever Frank would get him— probably by eight, so he had to find a way to kill seven hours. He hated sitting around bored. His older sister and brother had both moved out already, so he had spent most of the last two or three years being bored.

Lucas went back into the hallway and grabbed the broom and dustpan.

Out of all the things for a homeschooled kid to do on a Saturday, I clean my damn room.

He swept underneath his dressers and bed then started gathering all the garbage he had left on top of his dressers—there ended up being a whole garbage bag worth of trash. Once Lucas finished doing that, he opened his closet and planned to organize it, but paused for a moment when the chilly burst of air hit him. Even in a such a warm month, his closet was always cold.

He shivered as he stepped inside. There wasn't much of a mess—or anything—in here; he had a few jackets and a suitcoat hanging below two shelves of knickknacks and junks. Lucas had to get on his tiptoes to reach the topmost shelf, and shifting his hands between books and junk he hadn't seen in years, he felt the smooth surface of his forgotten photo album. It was warm to the touch despite the cold air that must've wrapped around it.

He went back to his bed with the photo album in hand, forgetting to shut the closet door. The air got colder all around him as he poked through it. Surprisingly, looking through it was a great way to kill time. He looked at photos from his childhood and reminisced about the good old days of being five. Sometimes, Lucas felt like a period in his life was gonna last forever, but eventually he'd grow up and realize that, unfortunately, that wasn't the truth.

By 5 PM, he was done looking through the photo album. He didn't notice the air had gone freezing all around him, as though the open closet door was an ancient fountain of chilling air. He put the album away, then shut the closet door. Maybe he'd add to it again one day.

Lucas went downstairs to find food. Mom and Dad were at work, so he was home alone. He yawned as he opened the fridge. He was tired and it seemed a thick trail of coldness had followed down the carpeted staircase and into the warm kitchen. He made a sandwich, then turned on the TV. All he could find were cartoons.

His phone rang before he was done.

"Hello?"

"What's up?" Frank asked.

"Nothing really."

"You do anything today?"

"Meh," Lucas said. "I looked at some photo album out of boredom. Reminisced, had some existential thoughts. I'm eating and watching TV right now. You?"

"Didn't do shit," Frank said. "I'll be over a little early to get you."

***

Lucas tuned out Frank for the whole drive, mostly replying with "Uh... yeah." to anything his cousin said. They arrived at the house a few minutes after the others— Micah, Jake, Janel, Lauren, and Paige were already inside.

He walked into the house with Frank. The air swayed between chilly and warm. It was unsettling—almost as unsettling as the way the house seemed to now tower over the rest of the homes on the block, as if it had somehow grown.

Lucas was almost shaking from his nerves; his face turned more red with every passing second until he got into the room with blue couches and saw Paige. Paige looked as beautiful as ever—her eyes were as fair as the moon and clear as the sun; he could only imagine how they'd glisten in the slight shine from the crescent moon outside.

Lucas sat a couple feet away from Paige, unsure if she wanted to talk to him again. Micah passed the blunt to Jake. Everyone was so... silent.

"Guys." Jake hit the blunt. "Is the S or the C silent in the word 'scent'?"

"Hmmm... okay, I'm not sure," said Janel. "And Jake, you can pass the blunt now... always hogging it."

"The C is silent in scent." Lauren said. "There's really no reason for the C to even be there."

"Well if the C is silent, then it would sound like 'sent'," Paige said, "but if the S is silent, it would sound the same with both."

Lucas laughed, "Um, airhead, it sounds the same minus either one."

"No, I think there's a slight difference," Paige said.

"Who cares?" Frank said.

Paige grabbed the blunt out of Jake's hand. "My turn!"

Lucas wouldn't have guessed she liked to smoke had he met her outside of here.

A few moments later the blunt was back with Jake. "So, how did the guys who made the first clock know what time it was?"

"Why must you constantly say things like that?" Lauren asked, slightly annoyed.

"You don't always have to take things so serious, y'know." Janel laughed.

"They're only funny sometimes," Micah said. "Most of the time they're lame, like 'if your shirt isn't tucked into your pants, are your pants tucked into your shirt.'"

"Is there a bathroom in here?" Micah asked.

"There's one by the kitchen," Jake replied.

"And it works?"

"Does it matter if it works?"

Lucas fidgeted with the hangnail on his pointer finger, "So whose house is this that you know it so well?"

"I don't know," Jake said. "I was looking for a new spot one day on Stone Road and discovered this place."

Micah was halfway out the room, "Okay, I'll be back in a minute."

Jake laughed. "I'm sure your palm can wait."

***

After ten minutes, everyone realized Micah hadn't returned.

"I guess his palm is extra good today," Jake said, trying not to laugh too hard at his own joke.

Nobody acknowledged it until about six minutes later when Lauren said, "Okay, I think I'll go check on Micah."

Frank replied, "Maybe he's just taking his time."

"I'll go see what's taking him so long," Lucas said, standing.

Janel was trying to pass the blunt to Lucas as he said this, but he didn't notice. She passed it to Jake because he'd ask for it anyway. Lucas went down the darkening hall that felt like demented demons with fangs for fingers hid in the corners. The white walls turned unsettling— their color didn't change, but it was as though something paper-thin lived beneath the paint job; something that was watching him. He was unsure of where the bathroom was when he got into the kitchen—then it hit him.

At first glance, it looked beautiful, how it contrasted with the linoleum floors. It didn't register at that moment that what he was seeing was blood. A slow stiffness built up inside of him as his mind began to realize what he was seeing. Micah lay there, with a yard-wide polka dot under him, and a dagger right through his chest.

***

It was late and everyone's parents were worried and frantic, but they had to be down at the joint Baylake police station and courthouse. Lucas was called into the interview room and sat idly until the interrogator stepped back in. The tone of the room—despite the bright lighting—was dark. The walls were gray and the only things in the room were the two chairs and the table. All of Lucas's fingernails were chewed down as far as they could go.

The interrogator was a tall and chubby man. His depressing eyes were intimidating—he looked like a man who had seen a lot and who was no longer surprised by this sort of a deal. Lucas didn't know why, but he felt guilty as he sat there, waiting for the man to speak. He was even more scared of him than finding a dead body.

"I'm Mr. Wilson," he said as he took a seat. His voice didn't match his face. "Don't worry, kid. I'm not gonna be as harsh or strict as you think I'm gonna be, just as long as you cooperate with me and answer all the questions truthfully." He took a pause, then added, "Ya understand?"

"Under-understood, sir," Lucas stuttered. The fear was written all over his face.

"Who was with you at the time of the murder, Lucas?" he asked.

"I, um, I-I dis-discovered Micah." Lucas paused. He didn't care for Micah—hardly knew the guy—but had to hold back tears. "The others in the house at the-at the time we-were my cousin Frank, his friend Jake, and hi-his friends Lauren, Janel, an-and Paige."

"Did you know him personally?" Mr. Wilson asked.

"I had-I had met him a couple of times before, but we weren't-weren't really friends, sir. He was my cousin's friend," Lucas said.

"So you didn't—so *nobody* saw or heard anything before the body was found?" Mr. Wilson asked.

"Well, none of us hear-heard or saw any-anything. We got a bit worried didn't come-come back, so I went to check on him."

"This is important, Lucas," Mr. Wilson said, staring into his eyes, looking for any hint of a lie. Lucas's hands were shaking and his head felt too hot. He wasn't sure what to do or how to act. "What happened next?"

"I-I walked in... oh God... I walked into the kitchen and, I don't know, I took a couple-a couple- a couple of steps, and I saw his body..." Lucas trailed off. He had never been around death and wasn't sure how to handle it. Most of the nerves had left him, but he was full of fright and confusion. "He was just lying there, he was stabbed, and I wondered to God how this could've happened when we heard nobody- nobody at all."

"Did anyone else see his body, Lucas?"

"Jake-Jake did, after I screamed and alerted everyone."

"Did anyone leave the room during the time Micah left?"

"No, sir."

"I need to know what you kids were doing in that house."

"Well, um, sir, I had um, gotten invited to... get... high..."

"So you guys broke into a house to get high?"

"I didn't know-I didn't know we were breaking into a house at first! I was-I was just invited by my cousin to meet his friends. I didn't know any details. I never really go anywhere, I was just tagging along."

"Just tagging along," Mr. Wilson said as though he did not believe Lucas. "Have you met your cousin's friends before?"

"Micah and Jake, uh, maybe twice before... or three times... I didn't know the girls-the girls until a day-a day or two ago."

"So this might be a hard question for ya then," he said, "but kid, did it seem like everyone got along? From what you saw? Do y'think anyone might've had it out for Micah? Could've had an accomplice do it?"

"Oh God, no. No. I don't-don't think any of them would've done that," Lucas said.

"Why not?"

"I just-I just don't think so. I haven't seen them all enough to know for sure, I-I guess. But-but no, I don't think any-any of them could've done that."

"Can you go over the events of tonight for me? From when you got there until now, just tell me how you remember."

"Frank called me and asked if I wanted to go smoke—"

"You told me you don't smoke. Why'd you get an invite?"

"My house gets pretty-pretty boring. Older siblings moved out, and my parents work most of the day, and—"

"Get on with it."

Lucas paused. He wasn't sure if Mr. Wilson was reading the terror on his face and was making a playful joke to calm him down, or if Mr. Wilson was serious.

"Nothing to do at my house. He invited me because he was being nice. He picked me up—I'm sorry, I don't remember what time exactly—and we went to Stone Road."

"Stone Road?"

"That's, um, what we call-call Lavenworth Road. It's a nickname.... So then the others arrived, and we walked into the house, down the hallway, and sat down and smoked. Micah needed to use the bathroom after a bit. Jake told him there's one near the kitchen. After close to... I don't know, twenty-twenty minutes? I went... I'm sorry..." Lucas swallowed the lump in his throat. "I went to ch-check on him because Lauren was concerned, then-then I walked into the kitchen. I saw hi-his body and went running, and then Jake didn't believe me, so he ran into the kitchen and then he ran out and it's a blur until we're here."

"Lauren was his...?"

"I think they had a thing. Not exactly sure what to call it."

"How did Jake know about the bathroom?"

"He-he said he found it the other day, I think. Prob-probably explored the house when he found it."

"There is no 'finding it.'" Mr. Wilson said. "The house was in the middle of town, not abandoned in the middle of nowhere. That house has been under construction for a while. The owner is living elsewhere until it's finished. I don't know how you guys managed to avoid seeing the construction workers—or how you managed to be completely oblivious to the renovations going on—but you need to stay away from the house. Understood?"

"Yes-yes sir!"

"I'm done asking questions for now. Is there anything else you want to say to me before I let you go, Lucas?"

"No sir."

***

Lucas didn't see Frank or anybody again for the next two days. His parents were keeping a close eye on him in the meantime. Now he was a week away from being done with homeschool, and his eighteenth birthday was tomorrow.

He had trouble focusing on final exams as the memories of that night replayed over and over again in his mind. His eyes shut and he's teleported there once again.

His mind is ticking—he remembers something, but he's unsure of what it is. He feels it again—the feeling of death—rising up out of Micah's carcass and entering his own. He wishes he could un-see it all but it's no use. The darkness all around him in the house begins to shake, and soon his head is swirling just like it did that night. His mind is trying to remember something, but he just can't for the life of him remember what it is.

There's a shake in his hands and a stutter in his knees as his eyes widen and a sickly feeling pierces his heart worse than the dagger that pierced Micah ever could. He remembers the way he turned around—morbid curiosity overtaking him and not wanting to look away... in fact, wondering what a dead hand would even feel like— and screamed, MICAH IS DEAD! OH MY GOD! SOMEONE STABBED HIM!

He'd never forget the way Lauren's eyes looked. He had no words to describe the pain he saw swimming in them; her soft, expressive eyes dulled down from a spring to a listless wave of water. The way her smile dropped looked like the way ripples thinned out and died minutes after a stone sinks to the bottom of a lake. Then, she said, "*What?*" in a hush. He hoped to never hear the emptiness in anyone's voice like that again.

His world in that moment seemed like a book with a gimmicky lenticular cover—it was one thing, then after the slightest tilt, it completely changed into something else. Everyone's expressions changed just as quickly. Jake pushed past him in a hurry.

In the next moment, Jake was back as if he'd never left the room. He couldn't remember what Jake was screaming, but it made the girls run out of the house. Lauren kept glancing over her shoulder, begging out loud to God for it to be a lie, a prank, a... anything, so long as Micah was still alive.

He could still feel how cold the handle on Frank's car felt when he opened his eyes.

His hand was cold to the touch, and there was still something he was forgetting.

***

Strong winds from a rainstorm hit across the windows of Lucas's room on the morning of his eighteenth birthday. It was still difficult to sleep and not be frightened; he found himself being too terrified to have his foot hang off the edge of the bed, something he hadn't been afraid of in eight or nine years.

Whoever killed Micah is still out there, and what if he is watching me? Or watching all of us? What if he's waiting beneath

*my bed for me, ready to crawl out like a madman, gripping that
dagger in his filthy, sweaty palm... I don't even want to imagine.*

But today was his birthday, so he tried to forget about
all that... but the ticking in the back of his skull wouldn't
shy away. He imagined a woodpecker hammering away at
the essence of his mind, and he watched it ripple away into
obscurity, ripple away into depressing soft waves...

*Something is not right. Something is not right. Something is not
right. Oh my God... something is wrong with me. What am I trying
to remember?*

Dammit, forget about it all. There's nothing you can do.

His eyes were heavy with dreariness all day. His sister
and brother—each having moved far away from
Baylake—came and visited.

Just relax. Your siblings are here. Have fun with them.

It was tough, his mind was strained, but he focused on
his birthday. Mom had to work, but they went to a
steakhouse when she got off. He had a fun time with his
family. Even if it was just for a little bit, Lucas Dyer was
happy.

But he was still trying to remember something.

***

The night he finished his final high school exam, the
thoughts of the night Micah died came pouring into his
mind again. It started subtly, then bloomed into chaos. His
mind begged him to remember—his body *needed* to
remember, but it just wasn't in him.

There was something that happened that he knew
would help put this case to an end.

*Did I see something? Maybe I heard it? If only I were there...
then maybe I'd... no, should I? No. I shouldn't... oh, but I need to.
I know if I just stand there again I'll remember it, I'll remember it
for sure. I'll know for sure what I heard or saw or whatever it was.
God, I can't believe I need to go back.*

He got up from his bed, then walked to the window
and overlooked the canopy of grey that seemed to hang
over the entire planet. The world outside his window
seemed as bleak as his mind was. Everything had lost its
joy. There was a void in him, and he did not know how to
handle it.

RING! RING! RING!

He almost ignored the call until he saw that it was
Frank.

"Frank? You all right?" Lucas said.

"Yeah, man. Yeah." Frank said. He had such a way
with words. "It's been... a week. Been trying to deal with
things... I'm sorry I missed your birthday."

"It's okay," Lucas sighed. "I don't care much for
birthdays. Just hard to get my mind off... the night.... I
finished my last exam today. I'm done with high school
now."

"Congrats," Frank said in a flat, dull voice. "Your
parents say anything about it?"

"Not a whole lot," Lucas said. "But they won't stop
hovering over me."

"Oh."

"Yeah..." Lucas said. "So, Frank..."

"Huh?"

"I... keep this a secret, okay?"

"Okay."

"Frank, I… I think I remember something about that night. I… don't know what it is." Lucas paused, took a deep breath, then continued: "I have something that's telling me—something in the back of my head—it's telling me that I saw something or heard something or know something but I don't know specifics. There's something there, Frank. There's something at that damn house that I'm forgetting, and if I just step back in, I *know* I'll remember."

"We'll go in the morning," Frank said with no hesitation or disbelief. "No way do I want to go there at nighttime again."

***

The sun was suspended in the cloudless sky the next day, when Lucas, Frank, and Jake revisited the house. It was lackluster, and the two windows by the back door seemed to be eyes staring at Lucas. It felt so alive that when his hand turned the knob and opened the door, he could've sworn he felt the door breathing.

Jake was reluctant to come along, but Frank said he wanted him here for this. There was a sense of panic all around the boys. They were on edge. If one of them even stepped on a crunchy leaf, they all jumped.

"What do you expect to find?" Jake asked.

"It better be something good, Lucas," Frank said. "Because I didn't even want to come back here, but it was better than letting you go alone."

"I don't know, guys," said Lucas, slightly annoyed.

Lucas didn't realize he was holding his breath until they stepped into the kitchen. His eyes darted all around, avoiding the area which once held Micah's body. When his eyes finally did land on that spot, it was hard to look away.

It was almost as if Micah's ghost was looking back at him. The air turned cold slowly and sent shivers throughout his body. A presence was with them.

"Is it—is it coming back to you?" Jake asked.

Lucas didn't answer. He played back those last few steps in his mind a dozen times. His mind cut out the part where he found the body a little more each time. He could see himself stepping closer to the kitchen, then in the next half a second, he was running and screaming.

Something wanted to be forgotten.

Lucas walked to the spot where Micah's body once lay; he could envision Micah's face as he kneeled down in the spot, remembering the... easygoing look Micah wore. There wasn't terror written on it, or even the smallest hint of fear. Micah had passed peacefully, despite the dagger that struck him.

It was starting to come back to Lucas.

I'm so close.

Dammit.

"It's almost coming to me," Lucas said. "Almost."

Jake's eyes turned angry. "Do you really know something? Or are you shitting us? I swear to God if there's something you aren't telling us..."

"No, no," Lucas took a step back. "I don't—I really don't know anything... but my head keeps telling me I do. The little voice in my head keeps bothering me about it... I think something might still be here."

"Something might still be here?" Jake repeated, confused.

"There was something in here," Lucas said. "I got this feeling... I can't explain it. Just trust me, please. I swear there's something we're overlooking."

"Lucas," Frank said, "I don't think being here is doing you any good..."

"The bathroom," Lucas said. "Can we check in there? Did he ever... did he ever make it there?"

Jake opened the door without any fear that Micah's killer could be behind the door. He hit a switch and the light from four lightbulbs filed the room. Frank entered next, then Lucas. The bathroom was normal—it was probably one of the only finished rooms in the place. Lucas moved the curtain that was already halfway pushed back. Nothing except a spider. Jake looked in the closet, but it was empty. Frank looked inside the cabinet that was under the sink. He examined every inch of it.

Lucas saw Frank's hand tracing over something.

"Did-did you find something?" Lucas asked.

"I found initials," Frank replied.

"What?"

"This part here at the top, it says 'V.H.'," he said. "It's a little dusty."

"Is this close enough to what you wanted to find?" Jake asked. He sounded like he was in a hurry to get out.

"Do you mind if we kee-keep looking?" Lucas asked.

"What more is there to see?" Jake said. "The inside of the toilet?"

"I wanna see the attic," Lucas replied.

Jake's hand trembled; he was a little on edge, and his breathing was heavy. "Whatever. This way." He led the way upstairs.

The staircase at the end of the other hallway—near the front door—twisted with what seemed like divine elegance as soft sunlight drizzled through frosted glass. The parts of the house that were unexplored by Frank and Lucas weren't as creepy as Lucas thought it would be. The house was gorgeous.

Lucas had pictured a dark, dusty attic in his mind, but this top floor was as high as the house went. The long, shadowy hallway didn't have a light switch that any of them could see, but shimmering light passed through the windows on either end. They could see for a little way, but the majority of the hallways was utter darkness—it was as if the darkness in the hall was evil, making the light come to a dead stop where they met.

"Where do you think the family's at?" Frank asked. "The one that they told us lived here but was staying somewhere else until it was finished?"

"No clue," Jake said. "Funny part is, I didn't even know that someone lived here when I found it. I didn't see any personal belongings."

"Were you trying to rob this place when you found it?" Lucas asked, surprised.

"No! I was just exploring and trying to see what I could find."

A door opened downstairs. Panic flowed through the Lucas's veins.

Jake whispered, "Stay calm," then crept to the stairs.

The cousins tiptoed behind Jake. It took all Lucas had not to throw up. Frank tried not to show how scared he was, but Lucas saw his hands shake and his lips turn white. When they got to the main floor, it was impossible to tell which door had opened. Everything still looked the same.

Jake turned back to them, nodded, then continued on towards the door.

"Hey!" a voice shouted from behind them.

Lucas whirled around to see a scrawny construction worker leaving the bathroom.

"Shit," Frank said.

They ran for it, but he didn't chase after them. Even without a chase, they couldn't have gotten to the car fast enough. Frank hopped into the driver's seat, Jake jumped into the passenger seat, and Lucas threw himself into the back of the car.

***

Something wanted to be remembered, and even while Lucas was at the Paytons' house the next day playing pool, it rang endlessly in his head. Jake was there too, playing video games against Janel and Lauren.

"I thought you were my friend!?" Frank shouted.

"And it's my duty as your friend to tell ya you suck at this,." Lucas said and sunk the cue ball. Janel and Lauren's house was in the nicer neighborhood in Baylake, one of those rich-people gated communities where the grass was always cut and everybody had hedges on the sides of their houses. Lucas hadn't expected that—he never had any clue that the girls were rich.

The basement had everything. Why had they gone to Stone Road to hang out instead of this place? There was a flat screen mounted on one wall surrounded by a mountain of PlayStation games, reclining chairs and beanbag chairs, carpeted floors, a lit fireplace whose flames were enchanting even from a distance, and of course, the pool table. Janel and Lauren had it made— their parents were loaded and never home.

Lucas set down the cue and walked towards everyone else, "I'm sorry, where's the bathroom?"

"I'll show you." Janel stood up, then led him up the stairs.

She walked down the hallway and showed him to the door before the living room. He put his hand on the knob, stopped, then looked back to Janel.

"Are you holding up okay?" Lucas asked. "I'm sorry, I didn't have your number or anything to ask. I feel bad since it's been... a while."

"No need to be so apologetic," Janel said nonchalantly, then whispered, "Between you and me... it might sound bad, but I never cared for Micah anyway."

Lucas didn't know how to respond.

"Oh?"

***

Paige was downstairs when Lucas got back. Heat suffused his cheeks when he saw her.

Come on, Lucas. Think of a way to talk to her.

He walked back to the pool table and grabbed the triangle rack and set it up for another game. Paige grabbed the other cue before Lucas even had to ask.

"I call breaking," she said.

That was easy.

Lucas wasn't a pool expert, but his older brother was, and had taught him how to use a cue. If there was anything that goofy Lucas was remotely talented at, it was this.

Paige broke the pool balls and sank a striped one into the nearest corner. She angled her cue again and sank another, then a third. Finally, she missed.

Dammit, she's better than I thought.

Lucas lined it up, then gave it a soft tap and sunk a solid blue in the pocket on the right corner. He tried for the next one—solid red—at an easy spot right in front of the pocket on the long side, and missed.

Paige laughed, "How did you miss that?"

"Quiet, airhead."

She sank the striped orange one while accidentally knocking in the solid red ball Lucas had missed.

"Thanks," Lucas laughed.

"It was an accident."

"No need to lie."

"Shut up." She lightly punched him. Lucas felt awkward and felt he was supposed to somehow make a move but she made him as nervous as a fly in a spider's web. She was gorgeous and he was a dork, he knew that she was an ocean wave carved into a glass statue and she didn't care for someone who was just shattered glass.

Eventually she had five balls sunk, Lucas had three. It was her turn, Lucas was nervous and his hands shook and he missed another easy (*easy as shit,* he told himself) shot because of it. Paige sank the 8 ball on accident.

"Fuck me," Paige said. "I let you win."

Lucas tried not to sound relieved, "Yeah right. I'd beat you again if we played a rematch."

"Whatever."

***

Lauren sobbed when the topic finally became about Micah. "I just keep thinking about him," she said. She rubbed her temple. "It feels like somebody swung a baseball bat across my head eleven times."

"What do you guys think happened?" Jake asked.

A chill ran through the air. Lucas rubbed his arms.

"Let's look at the facts," Jake said. "It had to have happened pretty soon after he got up. The fucker who did it had so much time to escape…"

"If he escaped," Frank said. Fear flowed through the room. They knew what he meant. "He could've stayed."

"It just brings us back to *why*," Jake said. "Doesn't matter much to me if he stayed and saw us, or if he left."

"Can we not… dwell on this?" Janel said.

"We need to know what happened." Lauren's voice cracked. "*I* need to know what happened."

"How did we not hear a struggle, though?" Frank asked.

Janel hugged Lauren tight, then whispered something to her before speaking. "I think he grabbed Micah from behind, put his hand over his mouth... you know the rest."

"It doesn't make sense!" Lauren cried. "We were in an unfinished house, minding our business, and what man is just gonna be there and ready to kill?"

The subject quickly changed, and within the hour, Lauren was no longer crying—in fact, she was smiling and laughing, telling some random story.

"So," Lauren said, "one time—"

"At band camp?" Jake interrupted.

Lauren rolled her eyes.

"One time, about two years ago, Janel and I come home from school, and we see our dog McKenzie playing with something. So Janel turns to me like, 'What is that?' so I go, 'I'm not sure.' We go up to her, and we see our neighbor's rabbit in our dog's mouth. We rush to get the rabbit out the dog's mouth and succeed with no problem, right? But then we notice two things: the rabbit is covered in dirt, and it's dead. So now we're freaking out, right? So Janel has this bright idea to force me to give a lifeless rabbit a bath. So I'm in tears as I clean off this poor rabbit, I'm just crying so hard I can't even see if it's even clean!" She was losing it, attempting to hold in her laughs. "I finish—oh man, I finish cleaning it, and I'm like, 'Janel, what now?' and Janel's like, 'Sneak it back in the cage!'"

She wiped her eyes. "The cage is already outside, so we sneak it in, and luckily, weren't caught. A couple hours later, we're outside relaxing, because it was a super nice day out, and we hear the most awful scream I've ever heard. Now we're standing up, all alert, and we look over to see what all the commotion is, and we see our like, seven-year-old neighbor crying at the rabbit's cage.

"So Janel being the 'nice' person that she is, goes up to our neighbor, hugs him, and says, 'Your rabbit died? I'm so sorry.' And long story short, the boy explains to us that it had died yesterday, and he buried it shortly after it passed… and that's the story of how our dog dug up a seven-year-old kid's dead rabbit and we put it back in its cage."

***

Janel and Lauren's rooms were adjacent to each other on the top floor. Janel's clothes decorated the hardwood floors in her room, and she was sure there was a laptop buried somewhere in the mountain of shirts and skirts. Lauren's room wasn't much neater.

Lauren shut her door and went to bed. Janel's snores drifted in through the thin walls. Lauren's eyes closed to lovely darkness and drifted away beneath the cold, soft blankets.

She was asleep within ten minutes, and did not hear the voice the faint, gravelly whisper that called out to her an hour later, "Lauren…"

"Lauren…" it called again, but she was oblivious.

"Laur… Lauren…" the voice called one last time in the still hallway, but it wasn't loud enough to wake up Lauren.

If only she knew what had happened.

***

The alarm rang at 7:05 AM. Lauren hit snooze then turned to her other side. She let out a small yawn as it rang again, then turned it off.

Ugh, so much to get done today.

She was halfway into the hallway when she saw Janel lying motionless on the floor just a few feet down, her bruised body decorated in blood. Lauren didn't notice her tears had begun to fall. She rushed to her sister and kneeled down beside her.

Janel had a contusion on her forehead, with blood from her scalp flowing gently to her eyes. Her t-shirt was ripped halfway off, and knife marks ran around her shoulder and led to her chest. Some marks were deeper than others, but most weren't severe—in fact, most were merely scratches. Whatever happened to her was more for torture than an attempt at murder.

Lauren's jittery hands felt for a pulse.

And she found one.

"Janel!" she cried. "Janel! Please wake up!"

"Lau—" Janel gasped, unable to open her eyes. Spit mixed with blood trickled out of her mouth.

"You're okay. Breathe. Just breathe. Open your eyes. Come back. It's okay. Whatever happened is over now. You're okay. Wake up. Please wake up. Don't do this to me don't do this to me, don't do this to me. I love you so much… Janel, come back!"

Lauren's eyes were so swollen with tears she almost fell over as she stood up. She went back into her room as fast as she could and found her phone. As she wiped away the endless rivers in her eyes, she dialed 911.

There was another terrible contusion found on Janel's head, and her foot was broken, but she'd live. The cuts would heal but the scars would never go away—they'd be a constant reminder of the monster who attacked her.

The hospital bed felt alien to her. The phone call with her parents had just ended; it'd be two days before they could get back from their business trip to Switzerland. Lauren stood at her sister's side, mumbling something as she held her sister's hand.

The door opened and a nurse led Mr. Wilson into the room.

"Hello, Janel," he said. "I'm Mr. Wilson, I was one of the detectives from a few weeks back. I believe you spoke to Mr. Heath. Are you doing all right?"

"Can't say that I am..." she said in a hushed voice. "Everything hurts and I feel dizzy."

Mr. Wilson turned to the nurse. "Can you bring her some juice?"

Janel said, "But I—"

The nurse was out of sight before Janel could finish.

"We feel this may be tied into the murder of Micah Gregory." Mr. Wilson turned to Lauren, "Lauren, if you'd please leave the room, I'd like to talk to Janel in private. And I'll need to talk to you too."

Lauren left the room and shut the door behind her.

"I know this is gonna be tough, but I need you to tell me what happened."

"I-I don't really know," she said softly. "I just remember being in the hallway and calling for my sister, but my voice would hardly come out. Next thing I remember is being in the ambulance... and as I'm there, I don't know if this is a real memory or if I'm imagining it, but I can just picture a shadow hanging over me, perfectly outlined in the flat darkness of my room. And I can remember the pain and-and-and I don't know. It's..." her voice cracked as she began crying. "Everything hurts, Mr. Wilson. Everything hurts."

"I know it hurts, but I need you to stay strong," he said. "If that is really your memory, if that is really what happened—and I know you said it might not be—then I need to know if you remember anything else about it. Any facial features? Did it say something? Anything?"

"No," she said, scared at first, then more confidently, "No. I can't remember anything."

"Your community is gated. Is there anyone in there who didn't like you, anyone you had trouble with?"

"Trouble with? No, sir," she said. "Not at all."

"We know how this person got into your house. There was a window open in the basement, with dirt on it and on the couch beneath it. There were footprints. We're doing all we can to find this son of a—"

"I forgot to close the window!"

"You don't have cameras installed, correct?"

"We were gonna, we just didn't yet."

"Convenient." He sighed. "Anything else you need to tell me?"

"No, sir."

"Then that's as far as I can get for now."

The nurse came back with orange juice.

Mr. Wilson left the room to find Lauren.

***

Lucas was drowning in sweat on that June morning when he woke up to his phone buzzing. It was Lauren. She hadn't called in a couple days—not since Janel had been admitted to the hospital. His stomach dropped with a godawful sickness.

"Hel-hello?" he said.

"Lucas! Hi." She sounded surprisingly cheerful.

"Sorry I haven't called," he said. "I wanted to give you some space. Is Janel okay? Are you okay?"

"She's... been severely hurt, y'know, but she'll be fine. I hope." Lauren said. "What've you been up to?"

"Well, uh... nothing to-to be honest. I haven't left my house since I heard the news."

"Well here's something you can do: you can visit Janel and me. Janel's been a little overwhelmed but I think she could use her friends. I'm inviting everyone right now."

"Should I—should I bring you or her anything?"

"No, Lucas," she said, a smile in her voice, "just visiting is enough."

"You never told me if you were okay."

"Yeah. Mostly. Actually, no... not at all. I'm scared."

"Me too, Lauren," he said. "But I'm here for you."

***

Room 916 gave off a desolate influence that hung over its door. On one side were Janel and Lauren, two frightened sisters trying to stay positive; on the other side, Frank, Lucas, Jake, and Jake's girlfriend, Valerie.

Lucas knocked on the door.

"Come in!"

Janel smiled wide, "Hey guys!" then her eyes fixed on the girl with blonde hair and mousy undertones. "Who are you?"

Jake's girlfriend grinned. "Oh, I'm Valerie. Nice to meet ya! I was with Jake when he found out his friends were visiting, so I just tagged along," Valerie said. "Hope that's okay."

"Well, it's nice to meet you, too. Sorry for the circumstances."

"How do you feel?" Frank asked.

Janel sighed. "Thanks for asking... there's just pain everywhere, but I'm happy I'm alive."

"What did the police say?" Frank asked.

"They know where the hell the person broke in—clueless on just about everything else," Janel said.

"I'm so sorry this happened," Lucas said. "They got you so easily, they got Micah with no problem... it's terrifying. Honestly? I'm scared to even wake up. I'm scared what can happen next. The uncertainty—this not knowing, that's the worst part."

"I get what you're saying, dude," Jake said, "but let's drop it."

A crinkled, faded blue envelope crawled underneath the door—it radiated melancholy into the already depressing room. A soft wind found its way through the shut windows and blew it even further into the room. It flipped to its other side. Nothing was written on it.

Frank handed it to Janel. Of course it was for Janel. It had to be—it was her room. She ran her finger through the flaps and ripped off the tape. She pulled out the note that was written on newsprint paper. The note said:

Janel.

Odd the things that happen when you're not looking.
There are darknesses in life, and there are lights. You are a light.
I still sit with you when you sleep.
I'm tempted every night to take you with me.
I know what happened to Micah. After all, I am the one who did it. And I'll tell you this: you didn't even have to leave the window open. I was already inside. I'm always inside.

If you want to know what happened to Micah, then have your buddies—every single one who was there that night—come back down to that house on Stone Road alone.

Your friend till the end—

Terror? Disgust? It was a toss-up. Everyone took a turn reading it over. Some people read it two or three times. They knew what they had to do.

Jake threw his hands up. "No. Nope. No way in fucking hell. I am not setting foot in there. Micah's dead. We know how he died. Does it matter who did it? What makes you think this guy'll even tell us? This straight up looks like a fucking damn fucking trap."

"I gotta know..." Lauren headed toward the door. "I gotta know what happened.

"Lauren, are you insane?" Jake asked. "You're crazy as hell if you're going down there."

"I've got to!" she cried.

"Fucking... dammit," Lucas said. "Janel, what do you think?"

"I, uh..." Janel paused to think. "I-I don't know. I mean if it makes this fucker stop... but who even says he *is* gonna stop?"

"I gotta do this. I don't care if you guys are with me or not. I'm going." Lauren opened the door..

"Lauren!" Frank called, but she was already far down the hall.

"Let's... let's go after her... fucking hell," Jake said through his teeth. "I am so sorry about this, Val."

They chased after Lauren and cornered her at the end of the hall.

"We can't do this, Lauren," Jake said. "It's fucking dangerous. This guy is fucking with us. Do you know what could happen? Besides, Janel needs you. You can't put your sister through this."

All his assumptions were logical enough but to Lauren, love outweighed reason and no matter what else he said to her, she wouldn't agree with him. She demanded to go to the house, and the others gave in.

***

Paige was waiting at the house when the others arrived—she looked like she knew they were arriving. Lucas and the others approached her cautiously and on edge. Lauren suddenly paced ahead of the group and rushed to the door. There was an uncertain sense around them—the disgust from earlier was amplified, and it was easy to feel terrified when the temperature around them kept swaying from a dull warmth to strands of nagging shivers across their backs.

Lauren paused in the doorway until everyone else caught up to her. She noticed, then moved out of their way. Once everyone piled in, a substantial wind slammed the door shut. They all exchanged fearful glances and looks, until Lauren said, "Do- do we just look around? Or…"

"Well, it was your bright damn idea to come here," Jake said. "You fucking tell us."

Lauren walked to the kitchen with a blank expression, then stood in the spot where Micah had been found. It was her first time even seeing it, but somehow she stood right there—something must have attracted her to the spot. There was a thin draft of air seeping out of the once-shiny floorboards that now turned into rotten garbage. The house was mutating—shifting—into something more devious than it ever had been. It was corroded, and the air began to tighten all around the teenagers.

Lucas took a step back, and noticed that the others also kept their distance from Lauren. Valerie bent over and picked up a note that was lying on the ground in the same sort of envelope that Janel had received her note in. She read it, then Lauren snatched it from her hands. Lauren's eyes traced the note and icy air traced the room.

Lucas could almost remember what he had seen the night Micah died.

"I-I…" Lauren gasped, not making eye contact with anyone.

She went back to the spot she was in, leaning over the counter, then said, "Micah."

Lauren walked out of the room.

"Lauren?" Paige called out. "Where are you going?"

"Micah," Lauren replied.

"What?" Paige asked, clearly confused. "Did you just say Micah?"

Lauren ran down the hall like an insane asylum patient escaping to the outside world for the first time in two decades. Lucas and Jake ran after her, but the others were petrified at the sounds that escaped Lauren's face, and the way her normally pretty eyes looked hellish when she glanced behind her shoulder after reaching the end of the hall.

Lauren beat them up the stairs and to the end of the upstairs hallway. She was encapsulated by the gorgeous rays of sunshine that entered the giant window at the end of the hall. She inched backwards with every step the boys took towards her. Her hands gripped the bottom of the window so tightly that her fingers turned pale. She pushed the window open with ease, then her eyes darted out to the concrete below.

"Lauren jus-just get back over here. Don't do this. Oh God, please don't do this," Lucas said. "Think of Janel. Your mom and dad. Think of your friends!"

Nothing stopped her. She stuck her right foot out, then her left, and fell with a smile. She landed on her neck— dead instantly, Lucas was sure. He and Jake flew down the steps and back into the kitchen. The sight couldn't have been worse. Paige was positioned in the same way Micah had been, her blood sparkling prettier than her innocent eyes that entranced Lucas ever had. Frank was hanging from the ceiling by an inch-thick rope; his eyes dangled sullenly from his skull, waving back and forth like a gentle wave that hits the shore. They followed Lucas around no matter where he stepped.

Then, in the hangout room where they had gotten stoned, came a tapping noise. Lucas followed it— everything else had stopped dead save for the beating of his own heart and the demented, infrequent tapping noise. His mind twisted.

He almost remembered.

Valerie Hart rocked back and forth in the corner of that room, hidden behind a couch. With every motion she made, the end of the crimson-covered knife in her hand hit the wall. Her hair was everywhere, her eyes were filled to the brim with tints of insanity.

"You-you did this?" Lucas cried.

"He made me do it!" Valerie shrieked and jumped at Lucas.

Lucas kicked her off with only a small scratch from her long nails that looked like they had grown since he had met her that morning. He ran, but she was quick and grabbed his shoulder. The knife sunk into the flesh of his lower back, then rose. A thin mist of blood sprayed Valerie.

Lucas screamed for Jake, but Jake didn't answer.

Where has he gone? Dammit. I didn't hear the front door open, I know that shithead is still in here.

Lying in a pool of Lauren's sweet blood and insides was the note that blazed strangely to the tune of the wind. Quickly, the pages were stained by the trickle that slithered from her shattered skull. The words disappeared, but not before he had a chance to see it for himself.

To whom it may concern—

By reading this, you are now responsible for the acts that have occurred and the ones still to come.

Pass it on, or the same fate comes to you as came to the others.

—Your friend, The Shape.

STORY TWENTY-TWO:

GHOST IN THE WIND

And he lies there, his head against the base of the tree and the blood from him falling soft against the pavement. I look upon his face and can see his death is upon him, and for a moment, his darkening eyes hold mine.

The icy air traces my lungs; my body is drenched in filthy darkness intertwined with chilling, sharp winds, and the natural sounds of the Redwick Woods fill my ears. The branches whistle and whack in the pervasive gusts of air.

I look back to the path from which I came and it is obscured in an instant—the wooden boards become twisted and rotten with an evil stench wafting along with wind. Oh God, that awful wind—there is something otherworldly racing along it. It's after me, and it's what killed my friend.

There is no going back. The other end of the path—the part I had not explored—still seems normal. The light is leaving the sky–it's either run from it or wait for it. I run, knowing I have an icicle's chance in hell at living.

The moonlight is my only advantage, but here in Redwick, the leaves grow so large and the branches are so plentiful that it almost acts like a ceiling, with random rays of light ornamented throughout it. The creature in the wind can't get me so long as I have *some* light.

A small, warm breath rides along the unseen wave of air and caresses the back of my neck. He's close and I need to move faster, but my feet are slipping out from under me. I can't end up like the others. Oh God, the others...

My hands grow numb, but it's just good to feel something other than emptiness. I don't know why I bother going on without my friends but I do. Every voice in my mind is telling me to lie down and wait for the sickly cold to consume me.

Or maybe it's just the monster in the wind telling me that. I can feel his crimson eyes fixated on my body, while he shifts like grim grains of sand and takes the shape of that damned, chilling breeze that's soaking into my skin and freezing me from the inside out.

I glance behind my shoulder, but all I see is the hellish void of gloom. It grows from a miniscule thing into a giant sea of obscurity—like standing in the middle of a dark well. All that lies behind me is total darkness. There is nothing to be seen. If I touch it, I am sure I'll drop dead.

I turn back to the path and push forward as much as I can; the path feels like jelly and the boards start to rise in cryptic, empty motions. Distorted bumps are scattered all along it. Every step is a chance to fall.

The air grows tighter. The end is coming, but the simple ray of moonlight I see just up ahead keeps me going. I long for it and the safety it promises. The darkness behind me is on my tail, and with every step I take, the earth behind me vanishes completely. There is only me and the hard-to-see path laid out in front of me.

I step on a bump and it shoots a knife of pain into my calf. The pain turns into white sparks of feeling in my thigh. My knees feel like rusty door hinges, ready to break off without a moment's notice. This is the end for me.

I sit down in pain—that is all I can do. The coldness is eating away at me, my sanity is drifting away, and the damned monster in the wind is ever closer. I try to massage the pain away, but it makes no difference. It increases and spreads upward. Tingles run all the way into my head, and I can feel my heartbeat in my throat and ears. My body convulses.

The monster in the wind is above me. The air grows so tight I can't move. I am a prisoner to invisible chains of bitter air. He drifts down a current and caresses my body. His nails—even colder than the air itself—sink into my flesh and a burst of warmth slithers along my back.

I try to find the monster's eyes, but my vision blurs and it seems that there is nothing around me but emptiness. My head spins as fast as a blink, and I think it will fall to the ground like a pencil rolling off a desk.

The nails leave my flesh and drag around me. The ungodly air seeps into my wounds, and the chill runs further into my very being and touches my soul. Everything about my existence is frozen. I try to breathe, but my aching lungs won't listen.

Snow begins to fall. It is strikingly beautiful the way the flurry of sparkles drift against black marble. The lack of light bothers me at first, but the snowflakes—seeming like a bag of stardust was torn open and spilled across the galaxy—is comforting. There is no better way to die.

STORY TWENTY-THREE:

FULL MOON

There was a curse buried deep within the soft but stony soil of the city called Carpenter. It rose every hundred years, and today—October 31st—was that day. Its presence sealed off the city from the rest of the world. For all its inhabitants knew, they were all that existed on the planet earth.

Carpenter was a lowly place of narrow streets, and the silence that hovered over it was always plentiful. It was homey, the sort of place where everybody knew who everyone was, even if they had never spoken. Everyone's front yard had at least one tree, which resulted in all the Carpenter blocks drowning in an ocean of cinnamon-colored leaves.

The high school let out early, at 2:30 PM. Sydney Dyer waited on the bench for Nancy Pearson, and once they met, they went on their way, heading south on Porter Avenue, to where Nancy lived. The fading green paint on the Pearson house made it stand out from most of the others.

"How do you not have a costume yet?" Nancy asked, opening the door. "Sydney, the bonfire is tonight!"

Sydney rolled her eyes. "I'm going as Nancy Pearson, the local slut."

Nancy turned the deadbolt and laughed. "Better than going as yourself—Sydney Dyer: the girl who's never had a kiss."

Nancy's room was the first door on the left at the bottom of the basement stairs; a tiny room, but cozy. The white, almost see-through curtains waved against her desk as the breeze filled the room. She had forgotten to close the window that morning.

"Kill me," Nancy said. "It's freezing."

Sydney set her book bag down next to Nancy's on the desk, then sat in the chair and yawned.

"I'm so exhausted." Sydney rubbed her eyes.

"Tell me about it," Nancy said. "I want to go to sleep forever."

"Yeah, your knees must be aching, too."

Nancy held back a laugh as she got on the floor, then reached under her bed for the costume she had hidden from her parents: an off the shoulder one piece that would reveal half her chest and would barely touch her thighs. One part of the dress tilted farther down than the rest.

"So you're actually going as the local slut?" Sydney said, looking at the outfit Nancy held up.

"No," Nancy replied, then slipped a hand back under the bed. She pulled out a pointed hat. "I'm going as the slutty wicked witch."

"You shit!" Sydney laughed uncontrollably. She laughed so hard it hurt and no noise came out. "How're—how're you getting that around your parents?"

"Simple," she said, "I'll go out wearing the hat, and I'll hide the dress under a robe."

"Leave it to Nancy."

***

Autumn chills emanated along the wind, and with it, the curse. They interwove and merged into one awful feeling that began to paint the town. Everyone could feel it coming—something bad was on its way, and it was moving toward the location of the bonfire.

Things were almost ready, but the party wouldn't start for another couple hours. Miniature jack-o-lanterns lined both sides of the steps leading up to 713 Wichmann Drive where April Mayberry lived. The front yard was one of the biggest in town. It was perfect for the bonfire. The logs were already set up in as neat a circle as they could make underneath the two towering trees devoid of leaves. Pumpkins with handprints carved out of them surrounded the inside of the circle. These would have candles lit inside of them later. In the center was the in-ground fire pit. In the frosty nighttime hours, it would look like a tunnel straight to hell.

Inside the living room, April was setting up the table of desserts that sat below the TV mounted on the far wall. Cora Green was helping to set up the fake webbings on all the corners of the room, nearly falling on her ass when she had to put one foot on the shelf that held family photos.

"Goddamn," Cora said. "Nearly slipped and cracked my neck, all for a party that won't even have booze."

"There'll be booze," April said. "It's—"

"More than one pint of vodka you're having somebody sneak in, April," Cora said.

April shrugged, then left the room to find more decorations. In the big mess of bags on the floor of her bedroom, she found the bag of forty-eight mini skulls.

"These'll do."

She brought them back to the living room and placed them around every table, the TV, the shelves, and even put one on top of the flowerpot. She dimmed the lighting just a little bit. Things were beginning to look spooky.

"What next?" Cora asked.

"Hmmm…" April thought. "Maybe putting some drinks on ice in the cooler outside."

As the girls spoke, the curse crept into the house like a spider crawling across its web.

***

The first guest showed up at 5:13 PM. The sky was a surreal swirl of pink and orange battling against the heavy blueness. The sound of crisp leaves trodden upon was music to everyone's ears. The air was lovely. Halloween night was going to be perfect.

Sydney and Nancy left Nancy's house around 5:30. Her parents weren't home yet, so she left in the slutty witch outfit, forgetting that her parents would be home in time to see her in the outfit upon her return. Sydney was just herself: she wore a long-sleeved blouse with a pink sweater and jeans that she wore to school.

"Aren't you cold in that thing?" Sydney asked.

Nancy replied, "A little," as if she didn't really care.

A boy was watching them from behind. He knew who the girls were and where they were going, but he was shy and didn't dare say a word. He was Jeremy the Mumbler, and he was who the curse had its eyes on first.

As the distance grew between the girls and him, his stomach got heavier and sickness spread as quick as a thought into his neck. His throat burned and he longed for water. His hands quivered and he slipped on a pile of leaves. Nancy and Sydney never looked back.

Instinct took over and he walked on all fours—his body still trembling with great pain—to the space between the houses. He heaved.

He looked to the sky; it was the last thing his eyes would see as human eyes. They too large for their sockets. In a flash, the sockets expanded, as his head disfigured and warped into an uneven skull.

Each tooth felt like it was being ripped out of his gums, but they were merely molding into fangs. Fur shot out of his skin like an ocean of needles—he felt every individual strand pierce his flesh like a knife. His body became too big for his clothes and shoes and they all tore off of him. He was a monster. He was a werewolf.

But the werewolves that came from the Carpenter curse were different: the change was permanent. They'd walk the earth as killers forever until death by fire.

Jeremy was hungry.

***

"Nancy, Sydney, glad t'see you could make it," April said.

There were already more people here than Sydney thought there'd be. She was already filled with social anxiety. She took a deep breath, then fixed her eyes on one of the miniature jack-o-lanterns. It was a little trick she had picked up, to focus on something and describe it to herself.

The jack-o-lantern had a long, crooked stem still sticking out of the top. Its eyes were small, and both of the pupils were looking to the upper right. The teeth were small, and its—

"Earth to Sydney," Nancy said from the first step. "Are you coming inside or not?"

"Oh." Sydney snapped out of it. "Yeah."

The Mayberry home was toasty. The ceiling lights were nearly off, but little red lights were hidden all around to give the living room a spooky aesthetic. Nancy grabbed a brownie, but Sydney suddenly didn't feel like eating. Her stomach hurt.

Sydney sat down on the only empty spot on the couches. More people walked into the house. This party was huge, and it was only starting.

"What's wrong with you?" Nancy asked. "Have a brownie or something. You've got nothing to lose, nobody's checking out your belly."

"Very funny, Nance," Sydney said. "I'm just not hungry. I don't feel good… you can go enjoy the fire, I'm staying in here."

"Okay." Nancy turned around and went out the door. There weren't chairs around the fire, rather just piles and piles of blankets with chocolate bars, marshmallows, and graham crackers all around. Nancy took a seat next to a guy she didn't recognize.

Nancy opened a chocolate bar, ripped off a square, then put it in her mouth. She could see the guy next to her checking her out.

Nancy turned to him. "See anything you like?"

"Yeah. Yeah, I do."

"What's your name?"

"Tommy," he said.

"I'm Nancy."

Nancy took him by the hand and led him down the side of the house and to the back yard. In the shadows, his hands weighed on her body, and hers weighed on his.

There was a growl in the distance too soft for either to hear.

***

Sydney looked around at the other partygoers and bit the ends of her fingernails. She took a deep breath and stood, rubbing her stomach, and smoothing her clothes. She got off the couch and went back outside. She grabbed the first thing her hand could find in the cooler—a Pepsi—then looked around for Nancy.

"Nancy?" she called, but she couldn't find her friend.

She sat down next to the people by the bonfire. It was mostly people she recognized, but nerves still played in her stomach. She wasn't very hungry, but she munched on a graham cracker while adoring the warmth blowing toward her.

At first, she thought the girl next to her in the witch's hat was Nancy, but it wasn't. She didn't recognize the girl with the mousy hair and eyes the color of forget-me-nots.

The girl smiled at her. "Having a fun night?"

"Somewhat," Sydney said. "I can't seem to find my friend Nancy. She's wearing a hat like yours."

"Hmmm…" the girl said. "Sorry, I haven't seen anyone with a hat like mine."

"It's all right."

Sydney looked away and grabbed another graham cracker. She was beginning to develop an appetite.

"I'm Mandy," the girl said.

Sydney looked back to Mandy and had to do a double take. She was positive Mandy had been wearing a long, black dress with horizontal black and white stripes up and down her legs… but now Mandy was wearing the dress Nancy had been in.

"That's—that's the same dress Nancy was in," Sydney said. "Who are you?"

"I told you, I'm Mandy."

"Did you do something to Nancy?" Sydney whispered.

"No, not at all," she replied. "I told you, I don't know your friend Nancy or where she went."

"Well it's just odd you'd be wearing the same outfit…"

"Yes, it's quite rare, actually." Mandy said. "It's the only witching outfit in Carpenter."

Sydney stood up. "Nice talking to you Mandy, but I should really get to finding Nancy."

"I'll help you look," Mandy said.

"No, really, it's okay," Sydney said, hoping the strange girl would leave her alone.

Mandy got to her feet, "The night's only getting darker, Sydney. You shouldn't go out alone."

I never told her my name, Sydney thought. *How does she know me?*

Sydney did not know which way to begin, so she just went to the right. And walked along the sidewalk with Mandy.

"It's so chilly tonight," Sydney said. "Awful cold."

"I don't mind the cold," Mandy said. "There are other things to be worried about tonight."

"Such as...?"

"Where your friend Nancy Pearson is, for one," Mandy replied. "And for another, the hundred-year curse."

"The hundred... I've heard of this before," Sydney said. "Somewhere at school, I think one of the boys—"

"Yes, yes," Mandy said. "And tonight is that night. Can't you feel it?"

Sydney did feel something rather odd.

"I believe so?" Sydney said, almost as a question.

"A lot of people tell the tale, and I suppose the tale itself doesn't really matter," Mandy said. "But what people may not know is what it does. Do you know what it does, Syd? Do you know what happens every hundred years?"

"I can't say I do."

"It's an unbreakable curse that's bestowed on a few unlucky ones," Mandy said. "Those chosen become a werewolf, and it's irreversible. The only escape—the only way to find peace—is death by fire."

"Frightening," Sydney said.

"Better hope we don't come across one," Mandy winked.

Sydney felt a lump in her throat. This time she was absolutely positive that Mandy's outfit had changed once more—back to what she originally saw her in: the long black dress with horizontal black and white stripes up and down her legs, and—

Where did her broom come from?

"You okay?" Mandy asked.

"I'm all right."

***

Nancy laid soft kiss after soft kiss down Tommy's neck, but neither of the two could ignore that faint, drowsy howl that drifted closer. She held him and he held her, their eyes locked into each other's, and shadows of fright played upon both their faces.

Then they laughed.

"Must be a movie or-or-or a—"

"-I know," Tommy said.

Nancy smiled, then went in for a kiss. The howl sounded again, and she shook, then pulled away.

"I'm sorry," she said. "It just sounds so... real."

"It's not," he assured her. "Do you want to go inside?"

They were pushed up against the brick wall of the house, below the patio that had one buzzing lightbulb lit. The yard was long and wide, and in the darkness, looked as though it stretched on for eternity into a damned abyss. Somewhere in the darkness was a tall tree, a trampoline,

mountains of leaves covering crabgrass, and a shed—
that's where the next noise sounded from.

CRUNCH! CRUNCH! CRUNCH!

Nancy and Tommy stared into the void, and although
they saw nothing, something saw them. It inched forward
in the darkness noiselessly, its yellow, demonic eyes were
spellbound on its target. It took another step, then—

CRUNCH!

Nancy took a step away.

Tommy looked at her. "Did you see something?"

Nancy shook her head, then ran. Tommy ran after her.
In the darkness, the werewolf that was once Jeremy the
Mumbler pushed his shoulders back, then jumped into the
air. He ran faster than a car toward the bonfire.

***

"Did you hear that?" Sydney asked Mandy, who was
now back to wearing the slutty outfit Nancy had worn to
the bonfire.

Mandy laughed. "Musta been a werewolf."

"I'm serious," Sydney said. "I think I heard a scream."

"It's Halloween, Sydney, there's lots of screams
tonight."

Sydney turned away from Mandy and ran back to the
house. She noticed Mandy didn't move, she just stood in
her place and laughed. The laughing stopped at some
point during Sydney's run, but she didn't notice when.

There was hysteria coming from the Mayberry
household—screams of pain and terror flooded the air.
Sydney only pushed forward because she needed to find

Nancy. She couldn't lose her best friend... not again. She ran as fast as her tired legs could take her, then paused in fright beside the firepit.

Her eyes filled with disbelief at the sight of fur drenched in blood and the sheet of torn skin drooping between closed, vicious jaws. The werewolf held April by her shoulders, its claws disappearing into her pale skin— then it turned to Sydney, tilted its head back, and let out a belligerent howl. Its eyes looked back at Sydney.

"Sydney?" a voice came from behind her.

It was Nancy.

Sydney turned around quickly, "Oh my God, Nancy, I thought I lost you!"

Nancy's jaw dropped and her eyes quivered. Sydney looked back to the monster that was spellbound on the girls. She desperately wanted to move, but her feet seemed attached to the ground. Fear had taken over and frozen her. Her heartbeat was the only thing she could hear—and she felt it in her throat and in her ears, that godawful beating like an aluminum baseball bat against tile floors.

The werewolf was a leap away, ready to pounce at Sydney at any given moment—that's when Sydney saw the rock Nancy threw at it. The werewolf took a step to the side, ready to run at Nancy instead. It growled.

"Oh my God Nancy what are you—"

"I'd rather it be me than you, Syd."

Nancy ran in the other direction but Sydney and the fire were still between her and the beast. The werewolf ran over Sydney, crushing her skull with a *POP!* It slid on her blood and over into the flames. His unholy, grimy fur was consumed in the spreading fire. His pathetic screams ran to the heavens but there was nobody that could come save the devil. Sydney was dead the moment he hit her, and her body was drenched in the expanding flames.

Amidst the screaming citizens, Nancy Pearson rubbed her warm, brown eyes then fell over from dizziness. All she could do was crawl across the cold grass and leaves, hoping she could get far enough away from the damned monster that was supposed to kill her instead of Sydney. Her whole body seemed to pound. The transformation was starting.

STORY TWENTY-FOUR:

EYES WITHOUT A FACE

The giant beech wood fence blocked off the yard from the neighbors she had never met—or even seen, for that matter. Of course she had always *heard* the people on the other side of the fence, but she had never seen anybody. The fence was much too high for a nine-year-old to see over, even on her tippy toes. There was, however, one small hole between two boards that she could peek through.

Stephanie Wernock sat with her back to the fence—she wondered why anyone would ever need such an ugly fence, or why it would wrap around their whole house like that—and pulled a daisy out of the small garden she had planted with her mother, Marilyn, months ago. She adored flowers, and these ones were her favorite.

Something passed over the hole in the fence. Stephanie ignored it. She hummed a soft tune as she dug her fingers into the dirt. An ant crawled up her thumb and to the back of her hand. She didn't mind, though—she liked bugs.

"Pretty," she said, holding the ant.

"You know what else is pretty?" a silvery voice from behind the fence said.

Stephanie jumped and squinted her eyes. She moved on all fours until she was far enough from the fence, then looked to it. There was a lady's palm covering the hole in the fence.

"I'm sorry?" Stephanie said. "What did you say?"

"I asked if you knew what else was pretty."

"Um," Stephanie said.

"Today is very pretty, Stephanie, isn't it?"

"I-I guess..." Stephanie said. "I'm sorry, I'm not supposed t'talk to strangers, ma'am."

"I'm just your neighbor," the lady said. "A neighbor's not a stranger."

"Why do you have such a big fence?" Stephanie asked.

"Why not have a big fence?"

Stephanie was truly at a loss for words. Her palms were sweaty and her stomach had a whole zoo running loose inside. This was a level of nervousness that the young girl had never felt before. Terror built up her mind. Why was the fence so scary?

"I dunno." Stephanie shrugged.

"You have a good day now, dear," the lady said.

Stephanie sighed in relief. "You too, lady."

"Oh, and by the way," the lady said, "next time you're wondering about the fence, just put your eye right here and maybe you'll know why we have it."

Stephanie nodded, as if the lady could see her.

All of a sudden, the palm was gone. Curiosity got the better of Stephanie, and her tiny feet moved before she even realized it—she was almost in a trance, standing in front of the peephole. Her hands rubbed against the wooden panels that cradled it, and her head moved slowly until she was inches away. She could only see the vague, shadowy outline of grass until she pressed her eye fully to it. She had done this before, and nothing was ever different. There was the rusty door that was always cracked an inch open, the tall grass that was never cut but also never grew, and a couple of rocks in front of the garage. Nothing was different at all, and there was no sign of the mystery woman.

***

Gorgeous June sunshine shone down upon the town called Radley the following day. All Stephanie could do was stare out her window at the neighbor's fence and wonder who was on the other side. The more she thought about it, the more the palm of the lady's hand—sweaty and reddening—popped into her mind. She couldn't describe it as anything other than nasty.

"Good morning, honey." Mommy walked into the room. "What're you looking at?"

"What's behind their fence, Mommy?"

"Fence? Oh, around the neighbor's house?"

"Yes, Mommy."

"Just a house is behind there, I suppose," she said. "Why do you ask?"

"No reason, I was just wondering," Stephanie said. "It just looks weird."

***

Nothing was new when Stephanie put her eye to the hole again. She was a little disappointed; she had wished to see the lady—or just anyone—but what chilled her to her bones was her mother's words from an hour ago, "Stephanie, nobody has lived there in years."

Once Stephanie took her eye away, the palm of the woman slipped back over the hole.

"Hey!" Stephanie said. "What're you doing that for!"

"It's a fun game," the lady said. "Makes you wonder what's back here, doesn't it?"

Stephanie paused. "Sure."

"You know there's a door at the end of the fence, don't you, Stephanie?"

"No, ma'am."

"Do you want to pass through and see for yourself what's going on here?"

Stephanie shook her head.

"That's too bad," the woman said. "There's something important back here."

"What's important?" Stephanie asked, a little amused.

The palm crinkled, and the lady spoke. "Something that only you have."

"Huh?"

"Forget I mentioned it, dear."

"I'm sorry," Stephanie said, "I don't know what you mean."

"It's okay, Stephanie. Go off and play today. I'll talk to you another time, all right?"

"Yes, ma'am," Stephanie said.

The palm moved away.

Stephanie did not look into the other yard; Stephanie went and played.

***

Abundant rain spilled over Radley through the night and never wavered, even into the morning, when fog filled up the ground and every glass window in the town was cloudy. Stephanie yawned when she woke up and then groaned—she hated this kind of weather, especially in the summer time when things were supposed to feel beautiful.

"Yuck." She stepped out of bed and went to the window. She wiped the condensation away with her shirt. Of course, the neighbor's fence was the first thing she thought of. For the first time in her life, she was infatuated with something; it was a feeling she couldn't shake—it was a really pretty fence, and the woman on the other side sounded so nice.

Who was she? She must be magic if mom and dad don't know about her. And if she's magic, what's she hiding over there? It must be wonderful.

She wished she could run outside and look through the hole on this rainy Sunday, but her father, Raymond, came into her room and reminded her it was time to get ready for church.

"Do I gotta go, daddy?" she asked. "I don't really want to."

He laughed. "Yes, you've got to."

"But Dad—"

"What're you gonna do all day, sweetie?" he asked. "Sit in your room and look at the ceiling? Now come on, put on your dress. Mom's almost ready and needs t'straighten your hair."

Stephanie frowned. She found a dress and her dad left the room. She wouldn't think of anything else during the sermon besides that intriguing fence and what could possibly be behind it. She wanted to desperately to know who the lady was and why she always stuck her palm there.

Stephanie had so many questions.

***

The next day was just as dreary. The fence looked even more mysterious, the way the rain from the sable sky hit it listlessly. Rain splattered against it, then plopped to the ground almost without care or motion.

Strange.

Very strange.

She watched it with great fascination, hoping she'd see somebody come in or out of the door at the end, although she could hardly see it.

You gotta leave eventually, lady.

Her legs cramped after an hour of standing. She hadn't even realized she had been there that long.

She crawled back into bed, desperately hoping that tomorrow would be a better day, and that she could figure out who was on the other side, and what the lady's words had meant.

...there's something important back here, the words wouldn't stop echoing in her ears. *Something that only you have.*

***

Tuesday was much, much brighter, but the backyard was still muddy and the porch was soaking wet. None of that mattered to Stephanie in the slightest. She shut the screen door behind herself, then marched down the steps.

Something important's behind it, and I'm gonna find it.

Stephanie put her eye to the peephole, then the palm of the lady slammed into it. Stephanie shrieked.

"Don't be scared," the lady said. "Good afternoon, Stephanie."

"Good—good afternoon."

"You really can't keep away, huh?"

Stephanie bit her lip.

"No need for that sad look, Stephanie," the lady said. "Here's something that might put a smile on your face. If you bring me a couple important things, I'll let you see back here."

Stephanie gulped, "I'm not so sure I should do that, ma'am."

"You can trust me, I'm your neighbor, remember?"

"My mom said nobody lives here... I don't think I should talk to you anymore."

"Oh, what would Marilyn know?"

"You know my mom?"

"Of course I do. We're not strangers."

Stephanie took a step back.

"The first thing I need's a knife. Any knife. Do you have any knives lying around, Stephanie?"

"I don't think I should be playing with knives."

The lady laughed. "You won't be playing with them, and neither will I. I just need them for... an experiment."

"I don't know..."

"Don't you want to see back here, Stephanie? Don't you want to see what's behind the magic fence?"

Stephanie stared at the palm. She *did* wanna know—desperately—what was behind it and who this lady was and why she was always staring at her palm.

"I do—I do wanna know what's behind the fence."

"It's nothing bad, Stephanie," the lady assured her. "So won't you please do it? For me? For your dear, dear neighbor?"

"Well... all right. I'll do it." Stephanie nodded her head, but felt pain in her stomach. "Any knife, you said?"

"Yes, any knife will do. Any knife will do."

Stephanie noticed the palm move. It was just a smidge, but it moved.

She went back into the house, careful not to make much of a noise. She did not want to risk her parents seeing her with a knife. Mommy was asleep, Dad was in the basement, but Stephanie felt that at any moment they'd both suddenly be there, catching her red-handed.

The tray of knives suddenly felt otherworldly. There was never a time where she cared what knife to grab, but this time she felt it needed to be important. She quickly glanced over her shoulder while her stuttering hand glazed over the one she picked out—the steak knife with the brown wooden handle.

Blood rushed to her cheeks and she almost cried, she felt so guilty.

Don't let Mom or Dad find out, don't let Mom or Dad find out, don't let Mom or Dad find out.

A floorboard creaked on its own and she nearly screamed. Her eyes widened and her lips twitched.

Let's go, she's waiting.

When she walked out the door, she was disappointed that the palm was no longer there.

"Hello? Where did you—"

The palm returned. Stephanie clutched the knife even harder.

"Aw, Stephanie, I see you've brought it, just like I asked."

"Mm-hm, ma'am," Stephanie said in a sweet, hopeful voice. "I did."

"Hand it to me."

The palm moved away and Stephanie was tempted to just take a quick glimpse into the other side of the mystical, wooden fence, but decided she'd be better off just listening. Stephanie put the knife through, but no hand grabbed it.

"Um?"

"Let it drop."

She released the knife and heard it land with a soft thud atop the uncut grass full of dew.

"What now, ma'am?"

"Rope. I need a little rope."

"Rope," Stephanie said. "Ok, ma'am."

"You know where to find it?"

"In—in the basement, I think."

"Good."

She went inside her house. Her heart skipped a beat as she started down the basement steps. Her whole body felt cold. She played excuses over in her mind, thinking of the perfect response for when her father would inevitably ask, "Where are you going with the rope?"

The basement was full of tools and wood and equipment on one end, the laundry room in the middle, and the man cave at the other end. The stairs led down to the man cave section first, and of course, her dad heard her climbing down the steps.

"Stephanie, baby, what're you up to, darling?"

"Playing."

"Playing what?"

"Do you have rope daddy?" Stephanie asked, then when he gave a confused look, she added, "I wanted to tie something together, some sticks. I'm building something."

He found her rope—just a couple feet—and sent her on her way. It was better than nothing.

***

"Here ya go, ma'am," Stephanie said, and slipped the rope through. She heard it plop.

"Mm-hm," the lady said. "Very nice, Stephanie."

"Is that all you need?"

The lady went silent for a moment, then put the rope back through. It was tied in a funny way.

"Huh?" Stephanie said.

"I made two spots for your wrists," she said. "Slip it on, and keep your hands behind your back."

215

Stephanie knew how outrageous that sounded. "Nuh-uh. I can't do that, ma'am. I'm sorry."

"Come on, Stephanie, don't you want to unravel the mystery? You'll be the only other person here to know what the secret is."

"I wanna know, but not—but I can't tie myself."

"Oh well, Stephanie, I guess you'll never know."

Stephanie gave in. She slipped her hand through one spot, put it behind her back, then put her free hand into the other. It fit perfectly, like it was made just for her. She let out a sigh.

"I'm ready."

"Excellent," the lady said. "Now, walk to the door."

Excitement and tension built with each step Stephanie took. She couldn't believe her eyes when the knob to the door began to twist. Stephanie ran in as soon as it opened, and a large smile spread across her face. The backyard looked just as it did through the peephole.

The door shut, and she heard the click of the lock before she turned around—and when she saw the eyeless face, it hit her. *That wasn't a palm.*

The eyeless woman raised the steak knife with a terrible grip in her deformed, arthritis-ridden hand.

"You've got something important," The lady said. "I need your eyes."

AUTHOR'S NOTES

There's some new content sprinkled in, but most of the content in this book has been published before. I sucked back then; rereading my old books made me cringe. That isn't to say I'm a master these days—especially since I published my second book of short stories just seven months prior to writing this book—but boy, did I improve.

I thank everyone who's made it through the book. I couldn't do this if it weren't for my supporters who bought this. I often look to my bookshelf and see creators whose work I adore, and I think to myself that I'll never succeed how they have, but I feel that if even one person enjoyed this book and found some escapism, then I've succeeded.

So thanks again for checking out my work. There's definitely more to come. If you'd like to stay up to date with me and my books, you can follow me on Twitter and Instagram, both @NasserRabadi13, and on my YouTube channel at Nasser Rabadi.